FOS
10/98

D0044768

MAPHEAD:
THE RETURN

DISCARDED FROM GMCO LIBRARY

Books by the same author:
MapHead
The Pits
Weather Eye

MAPHEAD: THE RETURN

LESLEY HOWARTH

CANDLEWICK PRESS
CAMBRIDGE, MASSACHUSETTS

For Wendy

"Our deepest fear is not that we are
inadequate. Our deepest fear is that
we are powerful beyond measure."

~ Nelson Mandela

Copyright © 1997 by Lesley Howarth

All rights reserved.

First U.S. edition 1997

Library of Congress Cataloging-in-Publication Data

Howarth, Lesley.
MapHead : the return / Lesley Howarth. — 1st U.S. ed.
Sequel to: MapHead.
Summary: MapHead, a boy with strange powers from a parallel dimension,
finds himself alone without his father for the first time and returns to
Rubytown to find his own destiny.
ISBN 0-7636-0344-9
[1. Science fiction.] I. Title.
PZ7.H83593Mat   1997
[Fic] — dc21   97-519

2 4 6 8 10 9 7 5 3 1

Printed in the United States of America

This book was typeset in Sabon.

Candlewick Press
2067 Massachusetts Avenue
Cambridge, Massachusetts 02140

CONTENTS

1

UP THE MULTI

MapHead stepped out of a ball of light and removed a tadpole thoughtfully from his mouth. He looked around as the glow settled slowly around him. At least he'd landed the right way up. The sign overhead told him that much.

LEVEL A said the sign. MAXIMUM HEADROOM 2 M (6 FT) MULTI-STORY CAR-PARK — TAKE CARE WHEN ENTERING.

There wasn't a lot else to see. Gloom. Concrete pillars stretching away into darkness. Orange box-lights overhead. And cars. Lots and lots of cars. One car had voices inside it. MapHead pricked up his ears.

"What *is* it? An' I want to *know*!" The little boy in the blue car was pointing right at him. "Looka that thing over there!"

"Maxie, belt up." The boy's mother started

the engine. The blue car grunted and roared.

"It's a *big* light, glowin' or something. An' I'm goin' to *zap* it, I am."

"Got your seat belt done up? I'm not sure you've done it properly." Maximillian's mother fiddled with Maximillian's seat belt. Then she looked up and saw the light. *"What in the world—?"*

A boy in wet trousers in a bursting ball of brilliance. That was what it was. A bright—a *very* bright—light. A boy bursting out of it, glowing gently, and—waving. At Maxie. In the multi-story car-park. Over SuperFare. On a Tuesday. The strange boy waved again. The grim-looking orange box-lights lit up the top of his head. A bald head, swimming with lines.

"I'm waving at him, I am." Maxie waved back. "An' he's *funny*, he is. Why is that boy funny?"

"Beats me. I expect it's a trick, don't you?" Maximillian's mother whitened, straightened, and suddenly pulled away. The Volvo jumped across E Deck and nosed down the exit ramp. She eyed her mirror anxiously. The apparition—whatever it was—waved to them all the way. Maxie waved back as they took the ramp, craning out of his seat belt to the last.

"An' I want to come back an' see him! An' he'll be here *next* time we come."

"We can hope."

She was brushing him off, Maxie knew. He watched her face in the mirror. When the sunshine flooded in at the exit where the money slotted into the ticket machine, his mother's face relaxed.

"I don't like these multi-storys much, do you?" She put on a smile that said *phew*. "Let's have some lunch. Like to stop at Pizza King?"

When the exit ramp had finally swallowed the waving boy in the car, MapHead dropped his hand and grinned. How nice people were. How friendly. It was only a shame they had had to hurry away. There were one or two things he wouldn't have minded asking the friendly looking boy in the car. Now he would have to find out for himself how things had changed.

The dimpled concrete ceiling of the multistory car-park stretched away in the gloom. LEVEL E said a bunch of big black letters. Map-Head shook some pond gravel out of his trousers. He should've known better than to kick off out of a pond. There were always going to be problems with gravel and tadpoles. It was just that it had come upon him so *suddenly*. One minute he was taking time out at the bottom of a deep and secret pool in southern Greece, the next he was thinking, *Rubytown.* No sooner thought than done. Not like before. Before he'd learned traveling properly, anything might have happened.

MapHead licked his pond-tasting lips. A drink would go down well. Olive oil, French dressing, anything. Where to get one? MapHead sighed. Things had changed a lot since he'd last visited Rubytown. *He'd* changed a lot since he'd last visited Rubytown. No Dad, no Mum, no traffic warden, instead a hulking great big sandwich of a car-park like nothing you ever saw *in* space or out of it. Glowing orange box-lights. Gasoline smells and shoppers. Strange marching letters ballooning over the walls. Someone had been busy with a spray can. MapHead frowned. Someone who couldn't—didn't—spell very well at all.

BUZ N'AG—back by yoor demand
Big Shout 2—Nik • Biz • CJ • Marky • Pete
SEE YA! wouldn't like 2 Be U when the
Triffs beat ya! Revenge is sweet—B. S.

What did it all mean? MapHead read the messages over and over. After a while his thoughts wandered. He'd been away. It was natural to find things confusing when he came back. MapHead traveled in bursts of light from one place to another, mostly in the spaces in between places and things, a subtle world where ghosts milled and slack dimensions shifted. The obvious world of people, places, and things made up everything you could touch and see and taste. The Subtle World made up all the things you couldn't.

MapHead sat on a car and thought it over. How long had he been away? In subtle time, a lifetime. In real time, a year, maybe two. The car-park was a funny place to pop up in. But it could have been a whole lot worse. He might have turned up anywhere. Better, by far, in a dim concrete sandwich filled with cars than in the middle of a field with either foot in a cowpat—or worse, the sewage farm. Even the *best* fix on Rubytown might have left him upside down in the cake shop, or wearing a hanging basket for a hat. He might have ended up in the dentist's chair just as he brought down his drill. In a math exam. Under a bus. On top of a bus. Inside a cow. Up a chimney. Down the pub. Half undressed in Woollie's Pik 'n' Mix. MapHead thought about all the awkward and unpleasant places he might have materialized in and then felt glad he hadn't. Luck, of course, came into it. But he was getting better, he knew.

AEROSOL DEMONS—
The Stoned Triffidz say Chill

BIG SHOUT 2—All that know me.
Art not vandalism—Respekt

Who *were* the Stoned Triffidz, wondered
MapHead. He hadn't known they existed
before he read their name on the multi wall.
He might never hear of them again in his life.
Or then again, he might. That was the joy of
traveling. Anything could happen.

Greece had been good. Especially the jour-
ney out. MapHead grinned, remembering the
round O mouths of the airplane passengers
when he'd waved to them from the wing of the
747. He hadn't been able to materialize too
well, on account of they were tearing along at
about five hundred miles an hour. Probably he
looked pretty faint—it might have been just
his smile, a bit like the cat from Cheshire in an
Alice book he'd read. It would've been a whole
lot easier *not* to have popped out of a sunburst
of light on the wing of a jet plane to goose
bump everyone in it, but MapHead couldn't
resist it. Neither could most of the passengers.
They goggled and pointed and steamed up the
airplane windows. MapHead had grinned and
waved. He guessed he'd beat the in-flight
movie hands down for watchability.

Yet his father had warned him sternly not to do it. Things like boggling airplanes were strictly out of bounds. Powers had warned him about a lot of things before he'd left, mysteriously and finally, for a space of seven years. Not one day more, nor less. Seven years would pass, whether they wanted to or not. Then MapHead would see his father again. The meeting place would be sent to him in a dream. A magic dream of his father. MapHead had better be ready. He'd better, warned Powers, be able to account for *anything and everything he'd done in this world or any other*. Powers's eyes had flashed dangerously. Power was responsibility. No taking advantage. Plus his task had better be done. Or MapHead would know all about it.

"All about what?" MapHead teased. He knew about joking now.

"All about the back of my hand."

"Yours and who else's?"

"The hand," said Powers fondly, "of the one who loves you best."

The one who loves you best. The sorry time of parting had come around more smartly than they knew. Now that the meaning of parting stood over them, deepening like a well, they had to go hollowly through it, MapHead knew, and come out again and go on. There

15

had to be partings, as well as meetings. Without partings there could *be* no meetings. Map-Head visualized his happy reunion with Powers in seven years' time. Then he blinked and said, "You know my task?"

"What about it?"

"I'll know when I find it, right?"

"Right."

"But why do I have to do it?"

"Because you're my MapHead, of course."

"But why?" MapHead persisted.

"You're thirteen. You've come of age." Powers gripped his son's mind with his. *"Power to move mountains is yours to do with as you please. What,"* Powers asked, *"will you do with it?"*

"Anything I like," MapHead returned happily.

"No," said Powers, "you won't. You don't understand. That's the point."

"The point of what?"

"Standing on your own two feet. I had a task once, too."

"You did?" MapHead swallowed. "What was it?"

"Something I never thought would happen to me. Something that made me what I am."

"What are you?"

"A space the winds howl in. A thing that

flashes from place to place. An awful thing. A lonely thing. Until I met your mother."

"No need to be lonely."

"Yes," said Powers, "*there is*. I told you. You don't understand."

"My task." MapHead thought. "How will I know when I've done it?"

Powers smiled. His teeth gleamed. "Oh," he said, "you'll know."

MapHead flashed his feelings around his scalp with all the sorrowful-sounding place-names that he knew. Usually he displayed cheery multicolored maps over his bald and uneven head. That was being MapHead. Maps of Rome had been a favorite—Rome had been home for a while before Greece—but maps of any place MapHead had ever seen or read about could suddenly light up his head with wiggly fjord coastlines or brimming inland seas, mainly whenever he was happy, and he almost always *was* happy. But now the mood was dreary. MapHead flashed up Sorrytown, God's Tears, Heartbreak Point, Port Regret, Meet-No-More, and Cape Farewell. Place-names were poetry to MapHead. It was all the good-bye that he knew. Maps were so much easier than words. Words had a way of getting muddled or meaning two things at once. MapHead sometimes got muddled

17

with words. But not as much as he used to.

Love. Trust. My son. Powers covered Map-Head's face with his hand. Then he glowed and thrilled. The air grew thick and heavy and burst into silver light. MapHead opened his eyes at last. His father had gone, traveling in lightning time to someplace in the Subtle World, that nonplace of dreams and ghosts and visions that fitted like shrink-wrap around the world of *here* and *now*. For the first time since forever, MapHead was alone. Seven years to prove himself, seven years to *be* as much as he could be. Seven years to find a task, a task that was MapHead's alone and might just prove as much as one lonely weirdo might have it in his empty heart to do. My funny heart, thought MapHead. My funny, empty heart.

MapHead stopped thinking when the car he was sitting on moved. The electric orange box-lights glowed, the car-deck stretched away. The woman with the trolleyload of shopping was busily transferring it to the car. That was the reason the car had moved. He hadn't seen her coming.

MapHead watched the woman incuriously as she filled up the trunk with carrier bags. He watched her fish her baby out of the shopping trolley and strap it into the car. She didn't notice MapHead at all, because he didn't want her to. MapHead had a way of being invisible if he wanted. It was a *subtle* thing he'd learned.

The baby crowed in its seat as the woman finished up. MapHead felt sorry for the baby. For some reason its mother had strapped it into a seat facing the back of the car, so the baby couldn't see where it was going. It was a nice baby. Ruddy, with brilliant dark eyes and a fetching vermilion suit.

MapHead watched as the baby's mother delved finally into the trunk. Then she clipped off with the trolley. He watched her park the trolley in the trolley park some little distance away, where Level E met the sun.

The baby crowed and pulled off a sock. It looked at MapHead, and MapHead let it see him. The baby stared, then chirruped, stuffing the sock in its mouth. *Bang—crash—clip—clip—clip*—it hadn't taken her long. Mrs. Shoppingtrip had parked her trolley. She was heading back to the car. She would jump in and drive away with her baby and that would be just about that. *My funny, empty heart.* MapHead watched the baby suck its sock. The baby crooned to itself. Its mother approached at a fast rate of knots. The baby crooned and kicked. Something about the way the baby flailed its red-suited legs for joy tipped the

19

balance in MapHead. He watched Mrs. Shopping trip rooting in her pocket for her car keys. Then he ran a tape-loop in and over his head, considering the likely echoes, past and future, of the move he was about to make.

Mrs. Shoppingtrip ducked into her car and started it up. At almost the same moment, MapHead slipped softly into the seat beside the baby.

EXIT RAMP AHEAD said the sign, as they spiraled down a solid flume of concrete into the fusty gasoline air. PLEASE HAVE PARKING FEE READY.

Mrs. Shoppingtrip had. She really was— noticed MapHead as he scanned the baby's brain and found it filled with juicy shapes and a large and nameless pinkness—she really was quite a good driver.

A NUMBER OF THINGS

The baby's name was Holly. MapHead scanned rapidly through anything and everything he knew about Holly and hollies everywhere, covering *Buddy Holly's Greatest Hits*, a history of Hollywood, the ad for Holly Homebaker's Instant Cheesecake Mix, plus the entire register of names at the school he'd once briefly attended—which introduced two more Hollys—in less time than most people could list them. But nothing much helpful came up, except lots of stuff about plants. *Ilex ilex (Holly), a berry-bearing evergreen mainly colonizing domestic woodland, tenacious in most deciduous habitats. Ilex aurora—golden holly (sterile). Ilex varigata—varigated leaves, low habit.* MapHead scratched his head. The things he knew about holly didn't seem to help much at all. "The Holly and the Ivy." When they are both full grown. Of all the trees that are *in* the woods, the Holly bears the crown. Trees bearing crowns seemed less than helpful. The baby didn't look spiky and green. Why name it after a plant?

The baby Holly lived in a room stickered around with perplexing pastel shapes. Soon after they got in from shopping, she had had to be unpeeled. A large dog watched closely as Mrs. Shoppingtrip laid her baby on a padded plastic mat covered with pictures of yellow and orange ducks. MapHead had— invisibly—sat down beside the large honey- colored dog, but the dog had moved away anyway. Probably it saw him, MapHead real- ized. Invisibility was a tricky thing to get right. It had to do with blocking the way people saw you—with absorbing light instead of reflecting it. Dogs didn't go for it much.

On the baby's chest of drawers were stick- ers showing a world of many things. Map- Head lay on his side and hopped in his mind from one to another, finally losing himself in all of them. The chest of drawers was white and unpleasantly shiny with flat white knobs and a built-in mirror on top. From his position on the floor, MapHead could just see the top of his head in it if he sat up as straight as he could. The picture stickers covered two of the drawers. They had on them a pig eating a chocolate eclair, Father Christmas, a toothy snake, a one-eyed monster in a spaceship, a strawberry ice-cream cone, a surprised octopus, a dog with a bone, a spaceman, a sun with sunglasses, a juggling clown, a sad-looking ghost, a mouse gorging cheese, a witch and a moon, lips blowing bubble gum, two teddies, a surfing frog, an Easter egg, a pink rabbit doing a handstand, a smiling python, the planet Saturn, a bee, a tarantula, a skeleton, a Halloween pumpkin, a parrot, another spaceship, an electric guitar, a birthday cake, a Christmas tree, two hearts pierced by an arrow, a Concorde, and a globe.

Phew. It reminded MapHead of something. *The world is so full of a number of things, I'm sure we should all be as happy as kings.* A poem. That was it. A poem from childhood days, way back in time. From a yellow-bound book in a cave. MapHead had spent a lot of time alone in a cave with a book, when he was very much smaller, while his father was off doing things you couldn't put a name to. Usually Powers had brought back food. And usually MapHead had eaten it. But it was food of another kind entirely that had kept him filled with pictures. Once he'd been old enough to discover the trailer park near the cave, there had been many more pictures, of course. Standing tiptoe against the trailers, MapHead had watched TV through the windows for hours. Mostly, he never got shouted at. Mostly, they never even saw him. MapHead had even seen baby-wipe ads. He knew about babies a bit. But he'd had *no idea at all* they had so many layers.

MapHead and the large honey-colored dog watched closely from different sides of the duck mat as the baby came unpeeled. It took a lot of doing, MapHead thought. He wasn't at all sure the baby liked it. He wasn't at all sure *he'd* like a wet undershirt pulled over his ears or his arms wrenched out of a cardigan. Mrs. Shoppingtrip tugged and pulled and fiddled. The baby kicked good-humoredly to start with, then several shades of upset crossed her face. Finally she reddened and cried— loud, then louder, as Mrs. Shoppingtrip ruthlessly unpopped her clothes. MapHead tuned in, distressed. The baby felt hot and prickly. Its mind filled with irritated shapes. Of course it was tired of lying on its back, having its legs bent for it the way they didn't want to go. Couldn't its mother *see*?

Off came the red suit. Off came the plastic wrapping under it. How many layers did a baby *have*? MapHead wondered. Inside its plastic wrapping the baby was all thick wet toweling and milky little legs.

"Weg. Watch out." The dog sneezed and shifted as Mrs. Shoppingtrip moved around it. "Weggie," she said, through the pins in her mouth, "get the cream for me, will you?"

The dog Weg crossed the room to a pink-lined wicker basket and clamped its chops around a smooth white pot. It recrossed to Mrs. Shoppingtrip, wagging its tail, grinning around the pot. The pot said PETROLEUM JELLY — BEST FOR BABY. Mrs. Shoppingtrip applied it vigorously to the baby's nether regions. The baby kicked and weed. MapHead felt quite ill.

The corridor from the baby's room took a plunge down a steep flight of stairs. Beyond a hall with a phone and a calendar and row of puffy-looking coats lay the herb-smelling kitchen, MapHead knew. He wandered downstairs to revisit it, having passed through once already in the rush to unpack the car and unpeel the baby upstairs. It was a lot like he remembered it. The kitchen looked a bit like a grocery shop someone had turned upside down to see what might happen inside it. All of the shopping that had taken up most of the trunk of the car had been brought in and dumped willy-nilly over the floor in crackly translucent-white bags that said SuperFare over and over. Out of the tops of the bags poked an astonishing variety of bottles and cans and loaves and blister-packs and three-for-the-price-of-two offers.

MapHead considered the shopping. Perhaps he might put it away. Mrs. Shoppingtrip was busy with her baby. He would be doing her a favor. It was a task, wasn't it? Not *the* task, of course. But it would add to the general sum of *helpfulness* in the world, MapHead knew.

First he filled up the dog's bowl with hard-sounding pasta shapes. WHOLE-WHEAT CONCH-IGLIE said the packet, maybe because they looked like little conch shells. MapHead tasted a few, rapidly analyzing the contents. Mainly carbohydrate. Some proteins, some sugars, some fats. Quite a bit of fiber, plus sodium present as trace. The dog Weg would be well fed on *that,* MapHead thought. After he'd crunched his way thoughtfully through all of the hard little conch shells that wouldn't fit into the dog's bowl, MapHead tipped biscuits into the muesli bin with an uneven sort of feeling it might not be *quite* right—then he put the Cocoa Pops where they looked as though they wanted to go. Was it *his* fault the tin was so full they cascaded out on the floor? He opened a cupboard over the kettle and a whole load of cookbooks fell out. MapHead turned them over. *Easy Pasta Cooking with Lisa Handslip.* *Cook Family!* by Lottie Reekie. *Pete Burns's Seafood Kitchen* by Pete Burns. *You Can Make Blood Sausage* by Caroline Quickly. He flipped through the pictures and stuffed the books back over the kettle. The people who wrote them had some pretty funny names.

MapHead was feeling quite at home in the kitchen by the time he heard the footfall on the stairs. He'd put away the shopping—finally, just about anywhere he could cram it—and improved culinary storage capacity no end. Plus, the fridge was sorted. MapHead had taken everything out and put back the things that really *needed* to go in, plus everything new that wanted cooling down a bit. Poor Mrs. Shoppingtrip hadn't a clue how to organize her fridge. It had needed sorting badly.

The footfall on the stairs reached bottom. MapHead held his breath; the door opened; Mrs. Shoppingtrip entered the room. She took in the changed kitchen slowly. A range of different expressions crossed her face, none of them quite equal, MapHead felt, to the scale of the improvements.

"Well, I must be going mad, that's all— who in the world's done *this*?"

Mrs. Shoppingtrip opened and closed her mouth. Then she opened and closed all the cupboards. Finally she picked up Weg's bowl of pasta and sniffed it. Then she sat down at the table and stared at her hands. After a long search for the tea bags she made herself a cup of tea. Then she examined her face in the kitchen mirror.

There was quite a lot—reflected MapHead, as he visited the room upstairs labeled JACK'S ROOM, ALL RIGHT?—there was quite a lot he had yet to learn about human behavior. The expression on Mrs. Shoppingtrip's face as she took in the kitchen improvements had been conspicuously lacking in approval. It had been, MapHead thought, an interesting experiment, but not one he was anxious to repeat. Probably it was the biscuits in the tin labeled MEASLEY or MUESLI. He'd known, at the time. That was what had done it.

JACK'S ROOM, ALL RIGHT? was a different kettle of fish altogether. For a start, it had the mark of someone MapHead knew and understood. There were cups and plates and books, apples and shoes and crisps in a comfy-looking muddle over the floor, plus a nest of clothes at the foot of the bed that looked as though someone had slept in it. Posters of men in dark glasses and big trousers with names like Kool Kutz, The Breeze, Prince TJ, and Dr. Dub looked down over Jack Allright's bed. MapHead guessed they were the same men on the slippery pile of CDs that sat in a corner of Jack's shelves. In pride of place on the floor lay a half-finished poster scattered with felt-tips. MapHead uncapped the purple and set to work. It wasn't until he'd completed coloring in the balloon-shaped letters someone else had started that he saw, with difficulty, what the letters actually said:

* HOT SOUNDZ *
* COOL RATES *
DJ BLACKJACK   PRINCE OF THE MIX

MapHead capped his felt-tip and looked at the message. It reminded him of the strange marching letters on the wall of the multi. Hot soundz. Cool rates.

DJ BLACKJACK   PRINCE OF THE MIX

It might have read BIG SAUSAGE FRITTERS RULE THE WORLD, for all the sense it made to Map-Head.

After he'd finished off the end of a stale Wagon Wheel he found stuck to a plate beside the telly, MapHead picked up a book and flipped it open. JACK BRADLEY STAMP—KEEP

OFF shouted childish red crayon inside. Map-
Head put it down again quickly. Then he
switched on Jack's TV. A picture of a spade
cutting into a lawn jumped up. Then the screen
filled quickly with a woman in a hair-
band and a green quilted waistcoat telling
another woman—rather bossily, MapHead
thought—how she could get rid of grass that
wasn't really doing anything by covering her
garden with cocoa-bean husks. They smoth-
ered weeds and filled up awkward corners.
They really were low maintenance.

MapHead thought he'd rather have any
amount of grass that wasn't doing anything
than the bossy-looking woman with her cocoa
husks. He switched programs and sat down,
settling happily to his favorite occupation,
channel hopping for anything and everything
funny, smart, or informative. Soon he was
watching penguins huddling grimly at the
South Pole, their penguin babies cozily
enfolded on their feet. *Polarwatch*—said
the screen over chafing icebergs and driving
snow—*Long Night of the Penguin*. The
program featured ice floes thick with penguins; penguins firing themselves like bullets
into mountainous seas; penguins hunched
together in their hundreds in walls against the
wind. MapHead moved closer to the screen,

his scalp crazed with polar maps. A million questions jumped up in his mind: *Why did the penguins stay there? How did they walk or eat or sleep with their babies on their feet? How could they stand around for weeks on end without food? Couldn't they go somewhere warmer?*

BAM! The bedroom door opened suddenly. MapHead jumped up. He hadn't heard anyone coming up the stairs over *Polarwatch— Long Night of the Penguin.*

A boy with startling orange hair burst around the door. He wore a bright red T-shirt and a flushed smile pickled with freckles and the kind of good-humored shine that said football practice after school.

MapHead dropped the TV remote and flushed a scale 1:5 map of the St. Lawrence Seaway over his head in a guilty panic. He forgot about penguins. He forgot about penguin babies. Most of all he forgot about *blocking,* realizing, too late, that the boy in the red shirt saw him.

MapHead adjusted his face the best way he could. He scrolled through what he knew about the game of football, taking approximately eight seconds to cover A to Z, inclusive. MapHead smiled wide, but not too wide.

Then he said, "Did you play football?"

The redhead stared. Then he nodded.

"That's good," MapHead said simply. Then he said, "Who are you?"

The redhead swallowed gamely. "I live here. *Who are you?*"

THE FAMILY STAMP

"Will there be hornets? In our picnic?"

"You like hornets, don't you?"

"And al-stuff?"

"And alfalfa. Yes." MapHead's father smiled down.

"*And* cactus milk? *And* those fries from the trailer park?"

MapHead was five. It was the most he'd said in a long while. Usually, he flashed up maps over his head by way of talking. That was being MapHead. So was learning — finally — to read, all on his own, on a rock in a cave with his father. His father hadn't helped much. MapHead had worked it out for himself, in place of anything better, like friends and family to grow up with. These were strange days, MapHead knew. His father, Powers, had put his traveling life on hold to bring him up in a cave, far from his mother and anyone, ever, remotely like him. Not that there ever was anyone like him, MapHead knew. Wasn't he unique? There was no one better with animals, that much was certain. Any animal alive would bend its neck and surrender, once it got the MapHead touch. MapHead had had a few pets. The only trouble was Powers. Powers had a tendency to melt small animals for dinner. But only the ones with no name.

The day the letters finally dropped into place and made sense, the day MapHead could really say he'd learned to read, was a day his father, Powers, had sniffed the California air and taken out a very special picnic. MapHead watched him pack it. Then he fetched his book.

Opening *The Snow Queen* proudly, at a well-thumbed place, MapHead read, " '*Thou art so powerful,*' *continued the reindeer,* '*that I know thou canst twist all the winds of the world into a thread, and if the pilot loosens one knot of it he will have a—*' "

"Favorable."

" '*—favorable wind.*' " MapHead snapped his book shut. "And I will be, one day, won't I?"

"Won't you what?"

"Be powerful."

Powers smiled. "More powerful than you think."

The picnic day held powdery clouds that grazed the tops of the mountains all around Mesa Rosa National Park. Powers chose a spot on a bluff-shouldered ridge, where pines marched up in the folds. First they ate hornets and avocado and biscuits shaped like bones, which Powers had pocketed in the pet store, and piles of vivid alfalfa by way of a salad. They washed it all down with cactus milk and root beer. Then they finished off with dog-eared french fries newly grazed from the burger-joint bins as an extra-special treat. After dinner Powers dozed in the shade of a flat rock shaped like a tabletop. MapHead took up rolling down the bluff. First he rolled a little ways to see how far he could go. Then he rolled right into the poison ivy and jumped up, howling quite a lot. Finally he rolled all the way down the bluff-shouldered ridge so fast he couldn't stop, faster and more and more hurt-fully, bringing sand and loose stones after him, till at last he crashed into something knobbly and teatime-sounding and fetched up smack against a man.

A big man with a beefy face. The beefy man looked at MapHead. He looked at his family's smashed-up picnic on its big red florid tablecloth. He looked at the burgers MapHead had rolled on. He didn't look too pleased at all.

"It's fine. 'Cept I hurt my arm." MapHead got up and patted a few things in place. "We had a picnic, too. With hornets and al-stuff and *everything*. On account of because—"

The big man's face darkened. He brushed off MapHead's hand.

"—on account of because I can *read*."

The beefy man got up. He leveled a fork at MapHead. *"Hey, kid. You're a dead man."*

"You silly." MapHead grinned. "Could a dead man do *this*?" And he made a map dance on his face. A map of Mesa Rosa National Park, obligingly centered on the ridge. Colors and outlines flushed across MapHead's extraordinary scalp as pigments triggered from cell to cell, faster than—as fast as—the thought.

The big man stared. Then he dropped his fork and did a dance of his own. MapHead always thought it was funny, looking back. The reason the man did a dance was, Powers'd heated the fork the man held in his hand with his distant, all-seeing eyes. That big fat man dropped his fork and started dancing around shaking his hand and forgot pretty quick, you bet, all about killing MapHead for rolling over his picnic. MapHead smiled, remembering.

The orange-haired boy in the football strip in JACK'S ROOM, ALL RIGHT? smiled as well. He remembered that big fat man as well as Map-Head—the whole unfolding scene—plus what Powers had said after. Jack cocked his head and listened to the thoughts inside his mind. *Blue Peter* blared on the telly behind him. He'd come home to find a baldy boy in his room. That was about all he knew. Except for the flood of memories. Someone else's memories, vividly remembered—so vividly, in moments they seemed like Jack's own. He'd forgotten about that picnic, he didn't know why. Forgotten how MapHead crashed into it. Forgotten he even *knew* MapHead. Jack smiled as it all flooded back. That man had jumped up so angrily. It wasn't so brilliant, Jack supposed, to have your picnic squashed. *All the same, it'd been pretty funny, the way that man had jumped around with a bright red face so even his family was laughing.* Map-Head smiled along with Jack as his—Map-Head's—memories unfolded inside Jack's mind. *That big fat man. With the hot fork.*

It had been easy to stop the orange-haired boy in the doorway; easy to empty his mind; easy to fill it up for him again with whatever

MapHead had wanted. What had been hard was being panicked into it in the first place. Interfering in someone's thoughts was decidedly iffy, MapHead knew. He wasn't, he knew, supposed to do it. His father Powers had said, *Don't take advantage. Respect.* But before he knew what was happening, he'd done it all the same. The meeting with Jack had been so sudden. What else could he have done?

Soon as they'd said hello, MapHead had taken a deep breath and dropped every memory he'd ever had straight into the flushed-looking redheaded boy's mind so that the redheaded boy would know who he— MapHead—was. It was so much easier than explaining. The door to the bedroom had said JACK'S ROOM, ALL RIGHT? Here was Jack himself. *Watch out, Jack. Coming through.*

Jack had stood perfectly still and taken it all in, just as MapHead had posted it all into his brain, red hot, firsthand, like his life was Jack's and Jack's life nothing but a dream. The day of the I-can-read picnic; a lonely childhood in a desert cave with storybooks; red-shadowed canyons and mountains; the tomato house he'd once lived in; his father; his mother, his brother; waterfalls, jungles, ravines; Rome, Greece, Arizona; his life in the Rubytown school, where he called himself Boothe; the spaces between worlds, where anything was possible—MapHead showed Jack everything so Jack would *understand*.

"I'm six now . . . now I'm *ten*. . . ."

MapHead concentrated fiercely. He was good at dropping pictures into people's minds and blending the edges in with what was there already. A pulse beat fast in Jack's neck. His damp hair stiffened and dried. His breath came shallow, then shallower, as MapHead poured impressions into his head, the way he knew he could without trying. When Map-Head had no more memories left to send him, he finally let Jack go.

"That's it." MapHead waited.

Jack swallowed. "Wow." A slow smile crossed his face. "Now I know who you are."

"Haven't I just *shown* you?" MapHead watched him anxiously. "Hey, Jimmy-Jack."

"Don't call me that." Jack shuddered, yawned, stretched, and peeled off his shirt to wash for tea.

"Jimmy-Jack. It's your name."

"Maybe it used to be. How did you know?"

"I can see it." MapHead looked into his eyes. Jack was OK. He shouldn't—proba-bly—have messed around with Jack's mind. But what was done was done. "I can see lots of things you can't. I can see Jimmy-Jack's your name."

"My name when I was a *kid*. It's Jack Bradley Stamp. Call me Jimmy-Jack now, you die."

MapHead paled. "Why would I?"

"It's just a line, don't worry." Jimmy-Jack grinned. "Want to watch me clean up? Smells like chips for tea."

They nudged each other in the bathroom like they'd known each other for *always*. Map-Head let Jack see what he was like, more than he'd dared show anyone ever before. In the hollow green chill of the bathroom, he showed Jack the prettiest maps he knew; maps with funny or rude place-names; maps within maps; sad maps, happy maps; maps that crept along his neck; maps that began at his temples in an ink spot and burst over his face like an April monsoon.

Jack watched MapHead's head in the bathroom mirror. How could a person make maps on his *head*? It was astonishing; amazing; unreal. Yet Jack felt entirely comfortable with it. He knew how the maps had started. He knew where MapHead came from, his innermost wishes and secrets, as well as the fine crack in the corner of the mirror that his father always told him to watch out for. He knew that

MapHead was odd and well traveled; unused to talking much; lonely, different, far-flung. It was as if he'd known MapHead for years.

Even so, it was amazing. "Wow. I mean, *wow*. I mean, like—how do you do it?"

MapHead shrugged. "How do you breathe?"

Jack shrugged back. "I just do."

"Same with maps. Except sometimes I do them when I'm angry."

"When you're upset?"

"I suppose."

Jack was solid. He liked MapHead, whatever. MapHead's heart filled. No longer as alone as a wet fish at a disco, but one among others, in a bathroom flicking soap with instant nearness to someone he'd only just met, MapHead unfolded like some secret bloom that had waited seven years for the rains. He would OD on the feeling in a minute. This was what it had felt like the time he knew his half brother. Jack Bradley Stamp wasn't MapHead's brother-in-blood. But somewhere there was a place they shared, a place where one thought knew the next, so that *who thought it* meant nothing so much as a taste shared, a smell well remembered, an echo sounding between them. MapHead's memories were Jack's now. It felt great to have someone *understand*.

"MapHead—Boothe, I mean."

"What?"

"Can I feel your head?"

MapHead grinned. "Feel your own head."

Jack Stamp pulled the plug and buried his face in a towel. "So why are you here?" he asked.

"That's something I have to find out. Anyway. Why are you?"

"Why am *I* here?" Jack found his face in the mirror. "Because. I don't know. I just am."

"Same here." MapHead squeezed the soap. It felt silky and smooth and green. He smoothed it—like a pet—in his hand. "I'm just here, and I have a task. And when I find it, I'll know. And what I'd like is, a bath."

"A bath?"

"Tonight. Please."

A bath. Jack Stamp grinned. With a gap between his front teeth he could've posted a letter through, he had a grin not easily forgotten. "If *that's* all you want, no problem."

"No," MapHead said seriously, "that's not *all* I want. But it's all I want for tonight, if you mind."

"If you *don't* mind," Jack corrected.

"No," said MapHead, "I don't."

MapHead hovered during tea. He soon got to

know the family — Mum, Dad, Lois, Jack, plus the baby, Holly. Elder sister Lois was interrupted by the phone at her second mouthful and spent the rest of the meal in the hall. MapHead sat soundlessly in her place. Jack grinned, enjoying the joke. Having a guest at the table no one noticed was a pretty strange experience. It wasn't that MapHead was invisible so much as *blocked out* in the minds of the family. They simply couldn't see the patch in their field of vision that MapHead took up, on account of he'd fixed it that way. The place where MapHead sat looked exactly like empty space to everyone but Jack. Jack watched his parents talk over and through MapHead, without a clue he was there. If it hadn't been so weird, it would have been funny. As it was, MapHead made faces. Jack threw a few faces back. Jack's mother stared.

Then she said, "Jack. Are you feeling all right?"

Jack shrugged. "I'm fine. Why wouldn't I be?"

"You're not eating much."

"So. I'm not hungry, all right?"

"No need to sound so cross."

"Well. I'd need, like, five hundred *hours* without food for serious nutritional depletion."

"What did you say?" Jack's mother looked at Jack.

"Just get on and eat." Jack's father looked up. "I'm not sure I like your tone."

Jack was about to tell his father he wasn't crazy about *his* tone, when suddenly he decided not to. Instead he made a *der* face at Map-Head. MapHead felt uncomfortable. Something strange with Jack. He didn't like the vibes.

Jack's father said, "How long has that girl been on the phone? Her meal's going to be stone cold by the time she gets to it."

"She can mike it. That's *her* problem."

Mrs. Stamp lifted the baby Holly out of her highchair and sluiced off her plastic bib in the sink. MapHead watched as the baby had her hands and face wiped very thoroughly with a washcloth. The baby put up with a lot, Map-Head decided. He looked at Jack and knew in a moment that Jack resented the baby. Map-Head looked away, chilled by what he saw. He drew closer to the baby. She smelled milky sour, of talcum and wee, plus another smell all of her own. MapHead warmed to Holly. Eat, don't talk. She had the right idea.

They passed Lois Anne Stamp in the hall. She'd been on the phone forty minutes. The conversation showed no sign of flagging at all.

"I know, I saw it, it's grim. She wears it, like, every time."

A pause. MapHead lingered in the hall to know what the call was about.

"No way. I went with him on Friday. And you know what he said when we got there?"

Jack motioned to MapHead. "Come on."

"I know, he's a beast. So why did she go?"

Lois covered the phone and looked at Jack. "Do you mind?"

"Mind you taking up all the hall and boring the—"

"Jack."

"—back end off everyone so no one else gets to use the phone unless they book it three days in advance? No, I don't mind. What's new?"

Lois made a face. "Oh. Excuse me." Then she continued where she left off.

"Sorry. No. Just an earwagger. Who did you think? Only Grimbo."

MapHead considered the top of Lois's head as he and Jack climbed the stairs above her. Lois was flame haired, almond faced, and considerably taller than he was. MapHead's ears burned. He would've given a lot to have been the telephone receiver. For some reason he couldn't quite fathom, he wanted to know what Lois was talking about more than anything else in the world.

"What is she talking *about*?" he asked Jack softly.

"Who cares?" Jack opened the door on his room. "She's always on the phone. She talks a load of—"

"Jack! Where's the *TV Times*?" Jack's dad called up the stairs.

"In the kitchen, last I saw. Dad!"

"*What?*"

"Did you ask Mr. Jameson?"

"About fixtures? I will, when I see him."

"*Gruesome. She didn't buy the trousers? Red or white? Oh no!*" Lois crowed under the stairs.

"I'm having a bath now!" Jack shouted.

"I needed to know that!" Jack's dad shouted back. "Let me know what color soap you use, will you?"

"*Oh, gross! That's totally—so when is she taking it back?*"

"I'll fax you!" Jack shouted.

"Fax you back!" shouted Dad.

"*She's getting the jacket as well? What does she think—he'll notice?*"

The conversational crossfire stumped Map-Head completely. Stifling a desire to go and sit in the garden among silent, forceful, growing things that didn't say *anything at all*, Map-Head wondered, for the first time, if he could live with the Stamps. They were pretty much like the families he'd seen on TV, only quite a bit noisier. He liked them. 'Specially Lois. And the baby Holly. Jack, too, of course. Three reasons to stay. Probably there was another reason somewhere. But three was plenty for now.

He watched as Jack Stamp ran the bath. A bath for him, MapHead knew. The water thudded into the tub in a satisfying way. A pulse beat slow in MapHead's neck. He watched his reflection rock gently in the bath water with Jack Stamp's reflection beside it. For a moment, his feelings blurred. For a moment, in place of Jack Stamp, it seemed to MapHead his half brother, Kenny, ran the bath beside him. Kenny turned to accuse him. *Why don't you come to visit? Why don't you stay with us instead of them?*

"I said, how hot d'you want it?" Jack Stamp stared. "Didn't you hear what I said?"

MapHead steadied himself. "Not hot. Just cold," he said.

"You want a *cold* bath?"

"Please."

"World of the Strange." Jack Stamp rolled his eyes.

MapHead looked at Jack uncertainly, not sure of anything now. Jack turned off the hot tap, then tilted his head and said, "You've got a brother somewhere around here, haven't you?"

"A half brother," MapHead corrected.

"But you don't ever hardly see him, because he lives with your mum and you live with your dad."

"That's right." MapHead smiled, relieved. It seemed so simple when Jack said it. He'd forgotten Jack knew—almost—everything about him now. Somehow it made all the difference. He felt calm and smooth and open, with all his nerve ends extended. He liked the bathroom a lot. It was cool and green and helpful to growth, and the window ledge bulged with plants. MapHead needed cool and green like a lifeline. Water, and then some quiet. He wasn't like Jack. These were the things, the life-sustaining things, he needed.

"Shampoo. Soap. Towels. Plus, there's all Holly's bath toys, if you're into plastic ducks. Mum'll bring Holly up in a while, you've got about half an hour," Jack warned. "Go on, then. Get in the bath."

"I will in a minute. Why?"

"Can you do maps anywhere else but your head?"

"I'm not a freak." The pulse in MapHead's neck quickened. "I'm just like you. I thought you *understood*."

"It's funny." A strange expression crossed Jack's face. "I feel kind of different myself."

"How do you feel kind of different?"

"I don't know. It's weird. I don't feel the same since you came."

Whatever the charge between them, it seemed to fill the room. The water in the bath waited coldly. A drip dripped—*plink!*—off the tap. MapHead felt sad and cruel, both at the same time, exactly the same way Jack Stamp did. Jack Stamp had seemed happy to start with. Something had gotten in the way.

"Why not tell your mum?" MapHead asked after a moment that seemed like ten.

"Tell my mum what?"

"Who I really am."

"You're joking."

"I mean, tell her I'm Boothe and I'm staying. That way I won't have to hide."

"You don't understand. She'll do things."

"What things?"

"Things like check with your parents. Things like call the police."

They both thought deeply for a moment. It would be about as easy to explain how a strange kid with a bald head popped out of nowhere and came to live in the house like the family cat as it would be to get the family cat to make a curry with all the trimmings.

"I suppose we could tell her you're a friend of mine or something," Jack said dubiously.

"Too bothersome," said MapHead. "I know another way."

"Oh," said Jack, "what way's that?"

"I'll get inside their heads. And make them think what I want to."

"You'll get inside my parents' heads?"

MapHead nodded. "Kind of."

"I thought you weren't supposed to interfere with people."

"I'm not," said MapHead. "How did you know?"

"I'm not sure." Jack Stamp closed his eyes. A drip dripped off the bath tap and plinked coldly into the bath. "I know a lot of things I never knew before."

"It's okay just sometimes." MapHead swallowed. *You're not supposed to interfere with people.* What had he done to Jack? "Just sometimes, if I'm careful."

"Hmm," Jack said. "I don't know."

"It's that, or else maybe I'll go."

"Don't go." Jack looked stricken. "Don't go, just—be careful."

MapHead submerged in the bath alone and fully clothed and let the water close over him a full twenty comforting minutes so that the baby Holly's bath ducks looked down from the soap rack only very slightly distorted by the still window of water between them. He thought many thoughts, which folded into one another. Chief among them was one that surfaced repeatedly and lived in the bath ducks' eyes. It was a watery, helpless kind of a thought for a boy striking out on his own, a boy with a task ahead of him.

The bath ducks looked down through the still, cold water and the thought ran on and on.

Dad. I'm not as good as I thought on my own. I feel weak and small, not powerful like I thought. I don't know what's right and what's wrong. I didn't know I'd have to choose all the time. Dad, I'm drowning, help me. I don't know what I'm doing. . . .

DON'T WORRY, BE HAPPY

After MapHead's bath was over, MapHead and Jack sat on the roof for a while. Jack's room was an attic room with friendly sloping windows that cracked open and swiveled all the way around if you wanted. It was pimps to get out on the roof.

"Pimps?" MapHead queried, raising what eyebrows he had. He hadn't actually said it. But still Jack picked it up.

"Easy-peasy." Jack colored slightly. "From when I was six. Easy-peasy-pimpsy. Pimps. Family joke. Kind of."

"Fine." MapHead smiled in a ghastly way. He wasn't feeling too well. What bothered him most were the feelings swimming around in the night air—feelings that clung to him like his wet clothes, with much less comfort about them. Somewhere beyond the sticklebacked town, his own family slept in their cottage. They would sleep a long time before they saw him. But it didn't make him feel any better.

The nightscape beyond Jack's garden rolled away to a misty moon over country hills far distant. The mysterious garden beneath him reminded MapHead of other gardens, other times, other moonlit meetings. Only this garden had new shapes, shapes MapHead penetrated with his night vision to find out the nature of things. The bulky-looking stuff running along the fence was runner beans, glowing with strength. MapHead could see the tips of the plants building cellulose and inching farther, higher. The runner beans, glowed green with manic energy. The mice in the hedge were tiny sparks of sapphire.

"So where will you live?"

Other gardens, other times, other friends. Mainly his half brother, Kenny. MapHead sighed. He'd promised, sometime, to return and say hi. Maybe he would, but not now. MapHead smelled the night air. What was his business here?

"Hey, Mappers. You with me?"

MapHead stirred. "What?"

"So where will you live?" Jack repeated.

MapHead thought. The warm light of

Jack's bedroom shafted out of the open window in the roof and lit up the side of the chimney. Muddled household noises rose—quite loudly—into the night. MapHead could make out the baby Holly grizzling in her cot, the sound of the telly, the sound of someone on the phone, the growl and grind of the dishwash machine he'd tried—and failed—to neatly stack with groceries.

"I'll prob'ly live here," he said carelessly.

"Where, here?" Jack looked around. "In my room?"

"*Here,* here." MapHead shifted uncomfortably. "Probably I'll sleep up here. Then I can see what's happening."

"You're going to live on the *roof*?"

MapHead got up. He'd been leaning against a smooth black disk beside the chimney. Map-Head considered the sculpted-looking disk. He tried to set it straight. Finely meshed and wonderfully smooth, it had the feel of an object of power. These things only cropped up occasionally. You had to *know* when you found one.

"On the roof," he said. "Why not?"

Jack had shuffled down into the gully where the chimney made a V with the roof. He lay on his back awhile, testing it out. He closed his eyes, imagining living on the roof.

"Can you shut that door? Thank you. And then you know what she did?" Lois. On the phone. The sound of her voice wafted clearly up from the hall. *"She only went and put pasta in the dog's bowl and half the shopping in the dishwasher and then—get this—the goldfish in the fridge! Of course, in its bowl. I know. She must've completely wigged out."*

"You're lucky, having a brother," Jack said suddenly. "I hate having sisters."

"Why?" MapHead asked, knowing Jack "remembered" Kenny, and everything else — or just about everything else — almost as clearly as he did.

" 'Specially Holly. I hate her."

"Holly's only a baby."

"So? That makes me *like* it?"

"And she filled up the muesli bin with biscuits, and all broken biscuits on the floor . . . and she doesn't remember doing any of it, and Dad says postnatal stress. . . ."

"Like what?" MapHead asked.

"The fuss. You know. The clucking." Jack put on a syrupy voice: "Oh, a late baby, they're always the best. It's just like starting over. You must be so thrilled. How much did she weigh? Oh, you poor thing. She didn't."

"JACK!" Jack's father's voice rose thunderously over everything else. "JACK, ARE YOU

UP THERE? WHAT'S UP WITH THAT DISH?"

Jack dropped deftly down through the sloping roof window onto his bed. He bellowed back down the stairs, "I don't know, what about it?"

"Has it fallen over?"

"How do I know?"

"Reception's rubbish! I'm trying to watch the film on TV Gold!"

"Nothing to do with me!"

"Can you see it out of your window? I only realigned that dish recently!"

"Looks okay to me! Maybe the telly's gone wrong!"

Jack waited, poised to slam up the window overhead should his father climb the stairs. Out on the roof was pimps. It was also Certain Death should his parents realize he did it. Instant removal to the spare room downstairs would follow as surely as — well, pretty surely.

Jack breathed easy as the living-room door slammed shut. Outside on the roof, MapHead appeared anxiously above him. Jack pulled the window open again. He looked up at Map-Head. "What?"

"Don't come up, it's not worth it," Map-Head said, the bedroom light throwing shadows over his face, his uneasy scalp swimming with lines. "Probably you'd better go to bed."

"You're kidding me. At *nine*?" Jack looked indignant. "You better put that dish back how it was. The round thing next to the chimney? It's messing up Dad's telly."

MapHead ignored him. "See this?" A map of Antarctica sat on his head like a hat with ragged edges. "What do you know about penguins?" he asked Jack sternly.

"Penguins? Why are you so interested in *penguins*?"

"I'm not sure, but I'm going to find out."

Jack looked at MapHead. The Antarctic Peninsula straggled over his face, the Weddell Sea pooled on his head behind it. The map was instantly replaced by another as MapHead's agitated scalp plotted a new scale every few seconds. Jack felt suddenly jumpy. It didn't take a genius to see the mood had changed. "Hey," Jack said, "it's all right."

"There's something I have to do." Map-Head struggled with himself. *What was his business here?* "I have to be alone. Not for long."

"It's cool. I'll see you later."

"Not for long," MapHead repeated.

"Not for long. Right."

"Don't worry, be happy."

Jack grinned. "Trust me, I will."

MapHead withdrew from the window. Jack

sat thoughtfully down on his bed. But Map-Head reappeared.

"Hey, Jimmy-Jack."

Jack pulled a face. "Hey, Jimmy-Jack, what?"

"Will it be all right?"

"Will what be all right?"

"Me. Being here. Will it work?"

"It's you and me," Jack said slowly. *"Just you and me, okay? Who needs anyone else?"*

MapHead thought. Then he said, "You won't watch me, will you?"

"When?"

"Just now. After I go."

Jack watched the Ross Sea pan over Map-Head's scalp. "Hey," he said, "why would I?"

But all the same, he did. When he stood up and peeped through the window, when he saw MapHead brighten like a taper, alone on the edge of the roof, and burn with a steady white light, he could hardly believe his eyes.

MapHead knew Jack was there. He knew how Jack felt when he saw him. He knew what would happen next, how Jack would react to it, how everything that *is* and *would be* would be very slightly changed, and still the world would turn. Maybe he shouldn't do it — especially not in Jack's view. Maybe he shouldn't travel in a flash somewhere his heart pulled him. Maybe he shouldn't flash back again. Maybe he shouldn't even think it.

Even as he thought it, MapHead felt the pull. There was nothing he could do. When the traveling life called, he had to *go*. Holding all of this and more in his heart, reaching the very edge of the roof, MapHead took the night air into his arms and launched himself off into space.

5

HUDDLE AT THE BOTTOM OF THE WORLD

The first emperor penguin MapHead approached shuffled away from him quickly, head down, flippers in, rocking from foot to foot, like a man with his legs tied together. The second took a peck at him. MapHead retired to a respectful distance in the lee of the wind and watched the huddle.

What had looked like a black standing mass as he'd flashed in over the ice shelf had resolved itself into penguins as he'd come closer. Lots and lots of penguins. Standing around in a huddle. In the bitter freezing cold. Now was the time to understand them.

But you couldn't ask a penguin. You couldn't say, "Excuse me, but why *do* you stand around in the cold when everything with a brain heads north?" North being warmer, south being colder still, MapHead reminded himself. That was the Antarctic for you. Here at the bottom of the world *everything* was upside down. Even night and day had decided to take a rain check and only clock in, turn and turnabout, for six months at a time together. Already the six-month-long night was deepening, the bitter wind singing more intensely. It would be a long haul for the emperors, huddling together for warmth; a very long haul till the Antarctic day finally lit the sky with overarching colors.

MapHead watched the penguins for quite a long time. Then he thought he'd join them. He made himself gray and blank all over. Then he approached the huddle. Close up, the penguins seemed larger than the ones he'd seen on TV. As big as a man around the chest, standing more than a meter tall, the emperors were on the move even as MapHead slotted himself into the wall. Huddling together to conserve heat—some three thousand or so in one group—the penguins shuffled constantly in a clockwise direction so that each took his turn on the outside. The wall of penguins on the outside edge of the huddle took the bitter brunt of the wind. MapHead felt it hit him. Inside, the huddle smelled fishy. But no fish had reached them for weeks. Ever since the females had handed over the eggs to the males and left, the ice-locked sea had grown further distant, the thought of food more remote. Not a penguin there remembered fish. MapHead searched their minds. Nothing but grit and instinct. The instinct to sit there with something round, approximately an egg, on their feet. Every emperor penguin's brood-pouch—the flap of skin designed to enfold and protect it—bulged with an emperor penguin egg. MapHead began to feel jealous.

At least he fitted in. If he were to move now, the wall would be broken, and the howling winds howl in. And that, MapHead knew, couldn't happen. The eggs must be sheltered at all costs. What the penguins were nursing on their feet was more precious, by far, than their lives, nothing less than the Future Nation of Penguins. It was awesome to join them. Even more awesome to hear the Antarctic night screaming and raging overhead. MapHead began to dream a dream as he shuffled from right to left with the cold, blank press of the penguins. He dreamed he laid a golden egg, an egg so precious he dared not show it to anyone. He nursed it in his brood-pouch and felt a glow when he thought of it. But one day it began to grow bigger. It grew and it grew and it grew. MapHead felt he was bursting. At last he rolled out the egg. Something was tapping inside it, something that wanted to come out. When it hatched and came out, the Something turned and looked at him. *What*—it seemed to say—*what d'you think you're looking at? Aren't I the picture of yourself?*

MapHead opened his eyes. The huddle stood far in the distance. A lordly ice shelf reared above him in spangled shades of green. He felt like Frankenstein's monster. Alone and very lonely, at the bottom of the world.

Ice mast-high came floating by
As green as emerald. . . .

MapHead sat under the ice shelf a long time while thoughts and dreams and half-remembered poetry rushed by him. *I want to fit in,* ran the pulse in his head. *I want to be one among others.* For the first time, some of the things his father had said came home to him with real conviction. Hadn't he—Map-Head—said, "You don't have to be lonely"? Hadn't Powers said, "Yes, you do"?

The power to do *anything* was incredible. Incredibly isolating. If all places were the same to him, where did he belong? *I want my dad,* MapHead threw at the uncaring ice shelf. Fathers and sons, like the penguins, stuck together—didn't they? Penguin dads didn't flash away and leave you to fit in—or not—

by yourself. They all stuck together in a wall. Penguin dads. Fathers and sons. The best dads in the world.

The wind whistled. The penguins shuffled. The ice shelf reared its lordly head in a million shades of green. MapHead felt a coldness touch him like nothing he'd ever felt before. The penguins would mate and roost every year, whether or not anyone saw them; the six-month-strong sun would rise and set like anything, whether it set on him or his shadow. Everything would go on, whether he did or not. That was its beauty and its strength. *His* life, his hopes, his dreams. Nothing cared, so he'd better.

He wouldn't end up lonely like Powers. He had life, and a task, ahead of him. Plus, he was just starting out. He could fit in anywhere, he knew it. Anyone could be extraordinary on an ice floe. The challenge was, to stay with an ordinary family. MapHead rose and jumped a mile in the thinking. On the highest point of the ice shelf, he looked down on the emperor penguins. Then he burned with longing for something warm and real. In the longing was the thought. And in the thought was the traveling.

BLACKJACK

MapHead opened his eyes. Shiny pink-toned dolphins revolved gracefully over his head, dipping and flashing coolly in the morning light from the window. MapHead watched them blankly. Then he turned over to face the drawers stuck with stickers of many-splendored things, which he'd noticed the day before. At diaper-changing time.

A pig eating a chocolate eclair, Father Christmas, a toothy snake, a one-eyed monster in a spaceship . . .

Morning in the baby Holly's room had the same smell as the baby Holly, MapHead noted lazily. Kind of smooth and scented and *comforting*. The baby Holly slept on in her crib, and above her the dolphin mobile nodded and flashed in the light.

MapHead considered the baby. She was, above all things, pink. Warm and pink and lovely, MapHead thought. He didn't remember exactly when he'd lain down on the floor beside her cot. He'd finally homed in on the only place he felt comfortable sleeping, sometime after he'd finished *traveling*. He'd been tired when he'd finally flashed in. When he'd finally lain down in Holly's room, dog-tired, penguin-stiff, he'd slept like—how did babies sleep? He'd slept, at any rate, like something slept that was very tired indeed. With the long night of the penguins fading behind him in subtle time, MapHead sharpened to the real world he had a foot in. Someone, sometime, had called him a bridge. A bridge between two worlds was really, he supposed, what he was. Except they weren't separate to start with.

MapHead ran a health check on himself. Apart from a temporary glitch in the absorption of fluids through his skin, probably as a result of exposure to sub-zero temperatures during the night, he appeared to be ticking over nicely. He felt perky and ripe for business, any business going. One thing he would settle this morning would be Mrs. Shoppingtrip. It was high time he and Jack's mother met eye to eye.

MapHead wrapped up his health check.

Then he ran a health check on the baby. While he was doing it she opened her eyes and gazed up at him, and MapHead experienced a falling sensation not easily forgotten. At last he understood. Falling in love. Except you couldn't fall in love with a baby.

Holly chirruped and jerked her arms and legs. She wore a pink zip-up outfit that smelled a bit every time she kicked. The nasty smell had something to do with a stain the color of toffee around her middle, where something that shouldn't have had leaked out. Holly didn't care. She kicked lots of times, then held her legs out stiffly, clenching and unclenching her fists, watching MapHead and, behind him, her dolphins turning lazily. MapHead grinned. Holly grinned back gummily. Map-Head saw, with amazement, that she hadn't a tooth in her head. He wondered how she chewed her food. There was a lot he didn't know about babies. Her father should, Map-Head thought, have someone to watch over her at night. The baby Holly was precious and should be protected. Anyone—*he*—could come in.

Breakfast was MapHead's first meal in the house as a proper guest of the family. He entered Jack's mother's mind and rearranged a few things as soon as she came into the kitchen. He dropped in a short picture story with friendly feelings to go, and let it simmer. Valerie Stamp's pale blue eyes grew vacant. Nothing happened for a minute or two. The dog Weg stirred in its basket. The clock ticked on the wall. Then Lois and Jack came in.

"Who's this?" Lois eyed MapHead coldly.

Jack did a double take. "This?" he said. "Who?"

"Your friend, of course. Doesn't he talk?"

" 'Course I do," MapHead told her.

Lois made a face. Jack grinned. She really did see MapHead. So, it seemed, did his mother.

"This is Pete Burns. He's staying awhile." Jack's mother took out breakfast things busily. She thought a moment. Then she opened the bread bin and brought out some muesli. "I'm going mad. More Cocoa Pops, Pete?"

MapHead motioned "no" over a bowl of chocolate milk. He especially liked the way the Cocoa Pops made the milk brown straightaway. He swallowed and smiled at Jack's mother. "Thank you anyway," he said.

Jack shook his head and mouthed, *"How did you do it? How did you fix things with Mum?"*

MapHead grinned back. *Pimps.*

"Why haven't you got any hair?" Lois sat

opposite MapHead and looked at him directly.

" 'Cos I don't want any."

"Oh."

Mrs. Stamp frowned. "Lois. Please. Mind your own business."

"Well. I'm only asking."

"If you must know, Pete lost his hair saving a puppy from a chemical accident many years ago." Val Stamp turned a shattering smile on MapHead. "I hope you don't mind my saying. *Such* a brave thing to do."

Lois's mouth twitched. "What kind of chemical accident?"

"The kind where puppies get caught in it," MapHead said stolidly. " 'S'long time ago now."

"So will it ever grow back?"

"It would if I wanted, but I don't."

That seemed to clinch it for Lois. She watched MapHead's every move over breakfast like she was storing up a blow-by-blow account to share with her friends, which in fact, she was. Breakfast was an irritable business. The clock on the wall, MapHead noticed, seemed to make everyone unhappy. Everyone checked the clock on the wall, then rushed around, looking grim. It would be a simple matter to fix it, MapHead thought. No reason not to be happy.

Lois was pretty grim anyway. It was the first time MapHead had seen her without a telephone receiver attached to her face. He waited for—what would be—the sunny warmth of Lois's smile. But Lois never smiled. Everything made her cross. Especially her school bag. She fought with it by the front door, her tightly bunned hair pulling her forehead, the cuffs of her coat interfering as she tried, for the final time, to introduce a thickly bound book entitled *Germany and the Industrial Ruhr* into a bag three sizes too small for it. She tossed back her head and jammed the *Ruhr* under her arm.

"I'm *sick* of this bag and I'm going."

Lois slammed out of the house. Jack's mother gave him a lunch box. Then she handed one to MapHead.

"I'm out of mayonnaise for sandwiches, so I've done you pickle instead. Cheese and pickle all right for you, Pete?"

"Pickle," said MapHead tonelessly. "Trouble; to be in difficulty. *In* a pickle. What is pickle?"

Val Stamp smiled. "Pickle's nice. I'm surprised you don't have it."

"I do," MapHead said quickly, getting the right meaning. "*A solution of brine or vinegar in which food is preserved.* I have tons of it. All the time."

On the way to school Jack seemed preoccupied.

At first they followed a growing gaggle of kids all dressed the same as Jack. Then Jack took a sharp left up a street everyone else seemed to be coming down.

"Won't I need blue clothes like you?" Map-Head asked.

"What?" Jack seemed lost in thought. His mood had changed since breakfast.

"If I'm going to school. Won't I need blue clothes like you?"

"Yes," Jack said testily. "Probably."

The morning seemed crisp and hopeful. A warm sun swam between terraced houses and flashed on the tops of cars parked endlessly along a main road that stretched away in front of them to a gray-walled garden somberly flanked with yews. No one walked behind or in front, MapHead noticed. The tide of blue-clothed boys and girls had entirely melted away.

"Why's your dog called Weg?" he asked suddenly.

"The Wegster?" Jack looked up. "He was Walter first. Walter, Watters, Weggie, Weg, Weggie Wegsford. Whatever."

"I see," MapHead said, not seeing at all. They walked on awhile in silence.

Then Jack said, "You did it, then."

"What?"

"Interfered. My mum. She thinks you're Pete Burns."

"Oh. Yes." MapHead nodded. "I made up a story in her head. About Pete Burns coming to stay. And his parents don't mind a bit, because they've gone away to Greece."

"Why Pete Burns?"

"Pete Burns's Seafood Kitchen," MapHead said simply. "I saw his fish-dish cookbook in the cupboard."

"You used to be Boothe once," Jack said, remembering. "When you came to Rubytown before."

"I used to be Boothe. Now I'm Pete Burns. When does it get there?"

"When does what get where?"

"When does this road get to school?"

Passing the gray-walled cemetery where the yews stood in rows like candles, a black-gowned figure overtook them briskly, paused, then crossed the road. MapHead stopped, confounded. The black-gowned figure flapped around a corner and disappeared, leaving MapHead with a vague impression of a face framed in white on top of a crisp black pyramid that cracked and snapped behind it as it went. It looked, MapHead thought, as it billowed around the corner, a bit like a manta ray. But manta rays didn't overtake people on their way to school. They didn't crack and snap as they walked. They didn't cross roads like swooping black crows. Mostly, they stayed in the sea.

Jack said, "It's only a nun. Nuns are—"

"I know," MapHead lied quickly. "I know what nuns are, kind of. It's just, I never saw one." And now it came to him what she—the nun—really looked like. Not a manta ray or a swooping black crow, but—"I didn't know they looked like penguins."

"They live up the road in a big old house with a garden and a pond. The pond's always full of tadpoles. I go up there, but they scare me."

"The tadpoles?"

"No, the nuns."

"They do look like penguins, don't they?"

"Not that again. Forget about penguins."

"I can't, now that I've seen them. No one should have to stand around in the cold with their babies on their feet."

"It's a joke, right?" Jack looked at Map-Head.

As they passed the space the nun had taken up just a moment before, MapHead caught a whiff of saints and martyrs. He tried hard to ignore the ghosts standing sentinel between the yews bordering the cemetery. Some ghosts tried to be showy. These were the kind to avoid.

"So where did you go last night?" Jack asked, more casually than he felt.

"To see what penguins do."

"So what *do* they do?"

"I told you. The dads stand around in the cold with their babies on their feet. And they never, *ever* leave them, no matter what."

"Then what?"

"Then the babies hatch out."

"I mean, what did you do after that?"

"After that I slept in Holly's room. I like Holly."

"More'n I do," Jack said darkly. "That used to be my room. I thought you were sleeping on the roof."

"So did I, but I couldn't."

"When you went—" Jack stopped. "You jumped off the roof. I saw you."

"I know. But it's not what it looks like."

"But I saw you jump off the roof."

"I didn't jump *off* anything. I jumped *into* something," MapHead corrected soberly.

"Into what?"

"Subtle time, what else?"

"What *is* subtle time?"

"Like dream time, only you're awake."

MapHead had a feeling dangerous things

were unfolding between them. He held Jack's eyes until Jack looked away.

"This is weird." Jack blinked rapidly, several times together. "This is seriously weird."

"I told you not to look, and you looked. You didn't have to know."

"So you're telling me you went all the way to—"

"Antarctica. In subtle time. I'll map it up if you want."

Jack stared. "Maybe later. Not now. Now we cross the road."

MapHead crossed the road behind Jack with a feeling of dawning understanding. He knew the place they were headed. He recognized the sandwich layer of concrete, the glaring overhead bulbs beaming orange light into dangerous-looking spaces, the many-colored gleaming tops of cars, the sign that said TAKE CARE WHEN ENTERING.

"Why are we going in here?" he asked Jack.

"Dump our stuff. Hang out. You got a better idea?"

"But what about school?"

"Stuff school," Jack said, with feeling.

Was this the flushed-looking winger who stayed late for football after school? MapHead followed Jack up the foul-smelling concrete stairway and knew, beyond doubt, that his newly altered friend was in trouble. Some of it—most of it—was his fault. In filling Jack in on his, MapHead's, past life, MapHead had opened doors in Jack's mind that Jack didn't know he had. Words like *you had no right* swam into MapHead's head. *Sorry* was in there somewhere. The meaning of breaking a golden rule began to tingle in his brain. Why had his father warned him not to interfere? Because there was a horrible reason not to. Everyone's mind was his own. You absolutely couldn't change it.

Newly mixed with exhaust, the morning air in the multi-story car-park smelled bitter and smoky and filled with things hostile to life. Cars stretched away in steadily filling ranks to the scabby-looking walls dividing every bay, walls that shouted the now-familiar marching letters that MapHead knew would spell out things he would never entirely understand. Jack considered them, too. He brought out a spray can and shook it. "See this? Dad won't miss it. Know who I am?"

"Who I am?" MapHead echoed, confused.

Jack Stamp popped the top off his spray can with the air of a gunslinger. Then he sprayed

!DJ BLACKJACK!
NEW NAME of OUTRAGE

in angry black capitals on a wall shouting monster *TRIFFS* tags. He stepped back to admire the effect. Then he added

BIG SHOUT 2
I wouldn't BU

Jack wrote it big and with meaning, shaking his spray can, enjoying himself with a new kind of glint in his eye.

MapHead watched uneasily. "But shouldn't we go to school?"

"We can do anything, right?"

"Right."

"So why would I go to school?"

Somewhere there was a reason. MapHead tried and failed to find it. Big—enormous—things were adrift with Jimmy-Jack Stamp, and he, MapHead, could hardly hope to explain them. But maybe he could contain them. Maybe he could watch and wait. Maybe things would get better. With his usual rising optimism, MapHead hoped the change in Jack Stamp would clock out with that day's traffic. Until then, he knew with dreadful certainty this was one ticket that could jam the machine. Largely thanks to him, the boy with the flame-colored hair was well and truly up the multi.

7

VALET PACKING—MAY I HELP YOU?

The day up the multi began quietly enough, with no hint of what was to come. Even Jack— though he wouldn't admit it—was bored. First he took off his school sweater and stashed it in his bag. Then he tied his coat around his waist and swaggered up top, where G Deck met the sky.

MapHead was glad to follow. The stench of exhaust made him tired of life. B Deck was filling rapidly. He found Jack leaning over the parapet that ran, two rails thick, around the top of the wall crowning the whole concrete-and-metal layer cake, seven stories high, which made up the car-park beneath them. MapHead looked down. Way below him, morning shoppers beetled around the market square like purposeful pinheads with

Important Things to Do. Unlike him and Jack.

"Starkey! Starks! Up here!" Jack whistled piercingly, then cupped his hands and yelled below, *"Surprise, surprise! Late again, Starkers? Take a demerit!"*

MapHead searched the pinheads below, some of them kids late for school. One of them—the one looking up now—was Starkers. In the time it had taken him to match the name to the face, Jack Stamp had scraped up a bomb, using a SuperFare bag and a puddle.

"Starkey!" Jack cupped his hands around his mouth. "You, Starkers! Cop this!"

Extending himself dangerously out over the parapet, Jack dropped the mud-filled carrier bag, craning out still farther to see it burst over Martin Starkey.

"Starkey! Starks! Tell it's raining?" Jack hooted and bawled like a madman.

It wasn't a good thing to do. Dropping things on people. Leaning out over the edge of a very high building in an excitable sort of way wasn't good either, MapHead knew. With rising anxiety, MapHead watched Jack. A tide of empire red washed over his scalp in the shape of northern India. He saw his hand going out to take the back of Jack's shirt in a safety grip. He couldn't help himself.

"Leave it out." Jack shrugged him off, eyes flashing.

"I only—"

"Well, don't. I can look out for myself. Who are you, Mary Poppins?"

MapHead considered this comment carefully. He desperately wanted Jack to slide back down off the edge of the wall and stop leaning out over the dizzy morning streets. Another centimeter farther—just a tiny amount—and Jack would drop like a piece of fruit off the multi and smash on the pavement below. Jack was in danger. What was he to do? What would the Poppins woman—whoever she was—have done in the same position? Jack's mother would want to know her son was here, seven stories high, on the topmost edge of the railings. Shouldn't he let her know? What should he do in the meantime? Shout? Faint? Eat?

"Mary Poppins says, *Keep In*," MapHead tried, sepulchrally.

"Give me a break." Jack eyed MapHead scornfully. "Anyway," he said, "if I wanted to walk all around the edge of this wall, you couldn't stop me."

"But you don't. Want to walk around it."

"Who says?" Jack looked at MapHead intently. Still looking at MapHead, he swung one leg, then the other, up onto the parapet. He pushed up his chest with his arms and brought up his knees.

"What are you doing?" MapHead asked quickly. "Lie flat, I should. Flat's best."

So far from lying flat, Jack straightened suddenly. Extending his arms he stood, with an effort, on the very edge of the parapet. "You could jump off this, couldn't you? Like you jumped off the roof?" Slowly he turned to look at MapHead. "And if I jumped off now, you'd have to save me."

MapHead flushed up the color of turkey wattles. "Please," he said, "don't. Please, don't."

Jack wavered on the edge. *"Wouldn't you? I know you can. You couldn't let me fall."*

MapHead's scalp plotted the Great Lakes in garbled detail. The Yucatán Peninsula cut into and overran them and spread like a flood down his neck. MapHead felt himself beginning to come unstuck.

"Please," he said, "you don't understand. My first time on my own. I don't know what I'm doing, and I can't have it on me, and I don't know what's right when you know you can choose and it's turned out fine today, how do you do? I say pleased to meet you and I don't like Jack going out where he might fall down, so then I say, 'Please, Jimmy-Jack, I want you.'"

MapHead stopped, trembling. Jack stared, then shuddered. When he opened his eyes again after, he seemed drabber and smaller, somehow. Somehow more like a frightened kid on the very edge of something he couldn't understand. He even took MapHead's hand when he offered, climbing wordlessly down and enfolding MapHead, without embarrassment, in arms that were suddenly shaking.

"Hey," Jack said, "it's all right. I don't know why I did that. I'm sorry, I'm really sorry."

MapHead squeezed Jack tight. Something relaxed inside him. It had been a close call, he knew, if Jack didn't. How close, he wasn't sure.

"You won't say anything, will you?" Jack said in his ear. *"You and me together. We're okay."*

MapHead nodded. Then he sat down. A new change had gripped Jack already.

Slicking back his hair, Jack considered G Deck with its ranks of family cars. His eyes swept over them shrewdly. A tight little smile lit his face. MapHead's heart sank. What next, after near death by falling? Jack Bradley Stamp changed course with the wind, a bit like

April weather. Sun and thunder together. No breeze, no clouds, no warning.

"Look at these suckers." Jack turned to MapHead. "All these happy shoppers. Now we're here, let's do some business. Are we ready to make some cash, or are we ready?"

"I don't know. *Are* we ready?"

"Ready, big time. What are we waiting for?" Jack said. He was actually rubbing his hands.

"Valet Packing. May I help you?"

For a while things went rather well. Map-Head had his lines off nicely. What he lacked in looks, he more than made up for in efficiency. Packing people's shopping into their cars for them was clearly a good thing to do. *Valet Packing. May I help you?* He had to ask them the way Jack had told him to. That way they'd want him to help. But why *did* he have to ask them that way? What did the formula mean?

"Val-ay packing. What *is* val-ay?" Map-Head asked Jack.

"It's where you look after people," Jack told him. "Like valet parking, where someone parks your car? Only we're doing valet *packing.*"

"I knew," MapHead said quickly, deeply

83

unsure of the difference. "It's just, I forgot for a moment."

The whole trick had been to convince shoppers that they—MapHead and Jack— were part of the SuperFare service. Once Jack had straightened his shirt and fished out his sweater for MapHead, they passed for staff no problem in their navy, green, and white. Luckily the SuperFare trim matched Hubert Sewell Community College colors. It was *pimps* cutting the Super-Fare logo off a couple of bags. Jack took his time with the edges. They had to look convincing or it wouldn't be worth them wearing them on their chests. Jack seemed highly focused. He even found a gluestick in his bag.

MapHead looked down at his SuperFare badge. Jack looked down at his. Then he looked up. "Let's go get 'em."

"How?" MapHead asked.

"Don't worry. Just do what I do."

MapHead soon got the hang of it. First you hung around the big metal elevator from the first-floor SuperFare store. Soon as the metal doors parted, revealing two, maybe three, loaded trolleys, you put on your best smile and said, "May I pack your shopping? Valet Packing?" Then you wheeled the trolley and put all their shopping in their car. Then they said thank you and left.

"Didn't you ask for money, you dope?" Jack shook his head over MapHead's latest—departing—client.

"Money? No. Did you?"

First Jack relied on tipping. Then he brazenly announced a service charge of ten percent of parking fees. Most people paid up, amazingly. But MapHead flinched a little. He hadn't realized Jack was charging. He'd thought, a little fondly, they'd simply been adding to the general sum of *helpfulness* in the world.

Jack took MapHead aside. "Look. It's better telling 'em straight out it's ten percent of parking fees than hanging around trying to grease 'em up, okay?"

MapHead had a feeling the guy in—official—SuperFare colors smashing empty trolleys together over by the lift might take a different view. He had his beady eye on them already.

"Maybe we shouldn't do this," he said.

"So you don't agree. So your cut can be less. That make you feel any better?"

Cutthroat businessman Jack Bradley Stamp was a tough guy to deal with. He only got tougher as the afternoon wore on.

"I'm hungry and I'm stopping." MapHead sat down at two.

"Here." Jack tossed MapHead a Twix, then a Crunchie.

"Where'd you get these?"

"I lifted 'em."

"Lifted them?"

"I borrowed 'em from people's shopping."

MapHead felt a wave of peculiar anxiety. That feeling again. Right and wrong, and all the stations in between. He opened his mouth, then closed it. Then he asked Jack, "Aren't you stopping for lunch?"

"Money doesn't eat." Jack scanned G Deck for clients.

MapHead dealt with the picture *that* conjured up. Then he said, "No. But you do. Anyway. Why are you like this?"

"Like what?"

"Cross all the time. You weren't cross before."

Jimmy-Jack shrugged. "Time is money. I know more things now."

"Why does knowing things make you horrible?"

"It doesn't. I mean, I'm not."

"*I* could be horrible if I wanted, except I don't," MapHead said earnestly. "Like my dad, when he—when he melts things with his eyes."

"Can you?" Jack asked.

"What?"

"Melt things with your eyes."

"Power is responsibility. No taking advantage. Respect," MapHead intoned, like a lesson. "You might want to think about that."

"I might, but I don't." Jack looked away, bored. "I was stupid before. Now I need money to travel and *do* things, all right?"

"I liked stupid."

"What?"

"The way you were before."

"Well, now I've changed. So you can get off giving me a hard time about it."

MapHead took refuge in his Crunchie. He'd seen the ad. *Thank Crunchie It's Friday.* He especially liked the honeycomb bit in the middle. Then he said, "What does Lois do at lunchtime?"

"What?"

"Your sister Lois. Where does she go to eat her lunch?"

"Who cares? She doesn't eat either."

"Lois doesn't eat?"

"She never sits down to a meal. She's always yakking on the phone."

The next few customers were the worst yet. An old gent with a bag Jack snatched, then thought better of it. A mother and kids with an overflowing trolley and a sarcastic laugh instead of money. A middle-aged woman who backed away when MapHead approached, a kindly smile on his face.

"Get away from me. You punkers."

"Punkers? It's Valet Packing." MapHead smiled some more.

"Well, you can pack yourself off," the woman said, waspishly. "Writing on walls. Vandalizing toilets. You punk types are all the same."

MapHead felt badly shaken. What they were doing seemed silly. The people who fell for it under the dim orange box-lights seemed silly. Maybe they liked having their cars loaded for them. Maybe it was the bad light. Maybe it was the multi itself, a world away from real situations. Couldn't they see they were school kids? That they should, after all, be in school?

One woman could. She eyed them both coldly and pushed her own trolley. "Shouldn't you both be in school?"

"He should, I shouldn't," Jack countered. "Don't you know? It's work experience week."

"And you are?"

"Executive Packing Operative. Cashier-to-Car Service. Personal Packing at a Price."

"You don't look old enough to me."

"You're the sixth person who's said that," Jack said smoothly. "Any more, and I'll start to believe it."

The woman looked at Jack. Then she said, "Well. Would you like to unload my shopping?"

"You don't look," Jack said coldly, "like a person who needs any help."

"Oh, but I—"

"Have a nice day."

Jack showed MapHead afterward the coffee he'd lifted from her bag. It wasn't that he wanted it; just that coffee was expensive. MapHead watched as Jack poured the coffee into a puddle. Then he kicked the puddle up the wall so that dark brown fingers of Continental Blend dribbled expressively down it.

"What did you do that for?" MapHead asked.

Jack Stamp raised his eyebrows. "Because I wanted to?"

The fight blew up out of nowhere. But somehow the coffee had brewed it.

"Let's go now. Shall we go now?"

It seemed like a good time to go. MapHead eyed the trolley smasher, talking now with a suit. The suit listened and nodded, looking at MapHead and Jack.

"This is good." Jack kicked the empty coffee jar. "This is different. Everyone should do what they want."

"You know you can't, Jack Stamp." MapHead

picked up the jar before Jack could smash it.

"Put it down." Jack waited.

"Supposing you smash this jar. Supposing someone steps on it."

"Supposing they don't," Jack said. "I want to kick things over. I want to do something *radical*."

"Radical," repeated MapHead. *"Thorough; complete; drastic. Upholding far-reaching change."*

"Whatever." Jack seemed bored already. "Anything—different, you know?"

"Revolution," said MapHead, *"a radical change*. Will you be like this tomorrow?"

"Maybe. What's it to you?"

"Some revolution. Valet Packing."

"What did you say?" Jack looked dangerous.

"I said, I'm going home to Holly." Map-Head peeled off his SuperFare logo with as much dignity as he could muster. "And I'm not coming back, so you know I'm horsy."

"*On* your high horse, you mean."

"And *you* don't stop me going when I want to."

MapHead walked hollowly across D Deck, head down, shoulders hunched, not avoiding puddles at all. Jack Stamp watched him go.

"That's right. Go home. Babies is all you're good for."

Babies is all you're good for. Jack Bradley Stamp's intended insult rolled around the multi and came back twice as nice. Remembering Holly, MapHead smiled. Jack could look out for himself. The baby Holly couldn't.

"What about your half of the take?" Jack shouted after him.

"Keep it. I don't. Want it."

MapHead dropped lightly into the stairwell, taking Levels D to Ground in a single swooping free fall. Once out on the street he quickened his step. The baby Holly needed him in a way Jack never would. If babies were all he was good for, MapHead thought with feeling, he was really quite good enough.

That afternoon MapHead found a reason to belong. Don't worry, be happy. It was really quite simple, after all. The baby loved him, he loved her—what else was there to know? Once he'd speed-read *Dr. Gillian's Encyclopedia of Childcare* his happiness was—almost—complete.

Everyone loved Holly—Mrs. Stamp's visitor; Mrs. Stamp's visitor's baby, Daniel; the dog Weg—everyone. Back at the house, the quiet of the afternoon settled around MapHead like a blanket. Home life agreed with MapHead. He could take any amount of

warmth and quiet and well-meaning household ghosts, like the biddy who lived in the
stairwell or the old man behind the bathroom
door. After he'd fixed the unsettling clock in
the kitchen so it wouldn't bother anyone ever
again, MapHead joined Valerie Stamp and her
visitor in the living room over two cups of half-
drunk tea. The babies made eyes at each other
and hurt themselves on things not obviously
dangerous and examined bright objects with
enormous care before dropping them. Map-
Head listened carefully to the two mothers. He
tried to pick up what he could from their conversation. Finding out all there was to know
about babies wasn't going to be easy.

"So, Peter—"

"Pete. Pete Burns."

"So. Pete Burns." The visitor smiled. "No
school this afternoon?"

"Pete's got leave to study at home," Mrs.
Stamp said automatically. "He doesn't normally go."

"He doesn't normally go to school?"

"That's right. Pete's very intelligent. He
doesn't really need to go to school."

"I shouldn't laugh." The visitor covered her
mouth. "I'm sorry. It sounds so funny."

"I suppose it does." Mrs. Stamp smiled. "I
don't know why it came out that way."

"I suppose that's the way it is. If he's so clever, I mean."

"He is. Very clever indeed."

No one said anything for a minute or two. Then the dog Weg appeared with a pot of cold cream in its chops.

"Oh, Weggie, no." Mrs. Stamp sighed. "Holly doesn't need changing."

"Isn't that your doorbell?" the visitor asked, following a dim *bing-bong.*

Valerie Stamp felt Holly. "I don't know, maybe I'll change her. Wegs, fetch my basket, will you?" She got up, looking harassed. "Won't be a moment. I'll just get the door."

"I can unpeel the baby," MapHead offered. He picked her up. She smelled. MapHead tried not to mind.

But when Jack came in, MapHead minded. When Jack Stamp came bloodily in at the door, MapHead minded quite a bit. He minded the way someone had turned out Jack's pockets and robbed him of every last penny he had, plus his door key; he minded the way they'd ripped Jack's shirt and thrown away his shoes; he minded the way they'd head-butted his nose so it wept all over his face. When he heard what had happened to poor old Jack Stamp when he'd not been there to save him, MapHead minded a lot.

SURFER MOE

"*You* look bad, you should see the other guy, right?"

"Right." Jack Stamp nodded, approving his version of events that afternoon up the multi. He had given a good account of himself. The other guy had come off badly and wouldn't, for sure, mess with Jack Bradley Stamp again.

"And you clumped him a good one," Map-Head repeated dutifully.

"Three good ones. I told you. Plus, I kicked him in."

"And you're not a bit sorry?"

"After what he did? Should I be?"

"So what did your dad say?"

"Lots."

MapHead went back to his book. "*Until emperor penguins are seven or eight weeks old,*" he read, "*they are kept and fed in their father's brood-pouch.*"

He stopped and looked at Jack. Jack's nose looked swollen and wonky. But he wouldn't be scarred for life. "So who was it that hit you really?"

"I told you. Big Shout 2."

"Who *is* Big Shout 2?"

"You'll see when we beat him in. I want you to melt him with your eyes."

"Melt him with my eyes? Why would I?"

"So you *can* melt things if you want."

"I can do anything," MapHead volunteered solemnly. "Anything at all. That's trouble."

No one said anything for a while. Instead of The Acid or Alkali Test, Jack wrote DJ BLACK-JACK COOLEST SOUND AROUND in his science exercise book in overlapping jumbo capitals. MapHead read his *Wonderworld of Knowledge*. Jack's bedroom seemed suddenly suffocating. The dishwasher churned in the kitchen downstairs over odd bursts of a soap opera from the living room as the living-room door opened and closed. The sound of the dog Weg scratching itself rhythmically—*thump, thump, thump*—on the kitchen floor rose steadily under the slap of Holly's bath water. Someone put the kettle lid on with a crash as Lois's confiding phone call wafted upstairs.

"He's completely bald with this white face with eyes like a fish, and he stopped the clock in the kitchen, and when Mum asked him, he said, 'I fixed it so you won't be unhappy at breakfast.' Yeah. Pete Burns. He's a trog. Do what? I couldn't. He might go mad or something."

"Don't mind her, she's a dipstick," Jack said.

"No," MapHead said, "I won't." But all the same, he did mind. *Pete Burns. He's a trog.* He got up after a moment. "I think I'm going to go in the bathroom an' help put Holly to bed."

After he'd helped put Holly to bed, MapHead lingered on in her darkened bedroom. It wasn't so dark, after all. He loved the pink light filtering in through the curtains. He talked to Holly a long time. He told her all about subtle time, the gopher he'd had for a pet, chariot races in ancient Rome, the way you needed to see a map once and then you could plot it forever. Holly chirruped through the bars of her crib and watched MapHead's face as he told it. Finally she forgot to kick and her eyes half closed and her fists twitched. MapHead watched her enter a subtle world of her own, the world between sleeping and waking.

Just then, Jack came in. "Mappers," he called, "you there?"

MapHead brought a finger to his lips. "Hey," he said softly.

"Hey, yourself." Jack rubbed his swollen nose. "Want to watch *Memory Maestros* with me?"

"I don't know. What is it?"

"This game show where people beat experts remembering loads of things."

"Things like what?"

"Stuff. Lists. Facts."

"I can do that anyway." MapHead straightened. "Diseases of babies include: allergies; asthma; bronchitis; bowel movements, obstruction of; crib death; cradle cap; croup; diarrhea; earache; eczema—"

"How do you know all that stuff?"

"*Dr. Gillian's Encyclopedia of Childcare.* 'There is no need to wash your baby's bottom every time you change a wet diaper. If he is dirty, simply clean him gently with cotton wool soaked in warm water—'"

"Okay, okay—is she asleep?"

"Holly? Almost. Come and see."

Reluctantly, Jack entered Holly's room. They both looked down on the almost-sleeping Holly. Her drowsy eyes looked without seeing, her fists twitched, expressions chased one another over her face and faded again like dreams without troubling her at all.

That, MapHead thought, was the way to be. Babies had a wisdom all their own. Holly's dolphins spun gently in the draft from the open door. The curtains moved very slightly at the window and shed their pink light over everything.

"It's like," breathed MapHead, "it's like, she's made of *pink*."

Jack looked at Holly's pink head; the way her pink fists clutched her blanket; the pink light bathing her cot. Holly turned her face, pinker still. MapHead was right. If pink was a thing you could shape babies of, Holly was made of pink.

Jack turned down her cover. "She's always wriggling down in her crib. Sometimes she gets covered up."

"She could get overheated." MapHead frowned. "It has been established that babies who become overheated are at greater risk of—"

Jack turned away. "See those?" He meant the stickers on Holly's drawers. "Those stickers used to be mine. Everything used to be mine. This used to be my room."

"Pretty old stickers," said MapHead.

"Yeah, well. I never come in here, do I?"

Jack was resentful of the baby—less so now, MapHead sensed, than when he came in.

He would do a little something for Jack, he thought. While the spell of pink still held him.

"Here." MapHead lifted Jack's arm. "Choose a sticker. Go on."

What do you mean? Jack looked at Map-Head. *What is it? Will something happen?*

"Go on. Touch a sticker. Any one you like."

A pig eating a chocolate eclair, Father Christmas, a toothy snake, a one-eyed monster in a spaceship, a strawberry ice-cream cone, a surprised octopus, a dog with a bone, a spaceman . . .

Jack's finger hovered—

. . . a sun with sunglasses, a juggling clown, a sad-looking ghost, a mouse gorging cheese, a witch and a moon, lips blowing bubble gum, two teddies, a surfing frog, an Easter egg, a pink rabbit doing a handstand, a smiling python, the planet Saturn, a bee, a tarantula, a skeleton . . .

—and chose. MapHead joined his finger with Jack's and the sticker image Jack chose filled both their fingers, their arms, their chests, their shoulders, their heads, their *minds.*

"Wow," Jack said, "oh, wow."

MapHead couldn't sustain it long. But while it was there, the surfing frog filled the room with its surfboard. It winked at Jack and showed him how it hung five, then ten toes over the edge, even though it had frogs' feet.

You know, Jack grinned, *I always liked you best.*

The surfing frog grinned back, plus it showed Jack what the other side of its T-shirt was like, which Jack had always wondered about, and it turned out the other side was just the same as the front, which said SURFER MOE. Finally the frog faded so that all that was left was its big old cartoonlike eyes; then they faded as well and Jack was simply standing there in the pink light of Holly's good-night time with his finger on a babyish sticker once his, in a room once his, in the evening, about eight o'clock. And that was all there was to it.

Jack put his finger away. "We're not going to talk about this ever, right?"

MapHead nodded. "Right."

He followed Jack out of Holly's room. Jack looked back at the sleeping room, at the curtains and stickers well remembered. Then he closed the door on it.

"Good, though, wasn't it?" he said.

Watching TV downstairs, they hugged the secret between them. During *Memory Maestros*—MapHead turned out genius at remembering things, beating all the maestros hands down, especially the ones trying place-names—during *Memory Maestros,* Mr. Stamp seemed more talkative than usual.

"So," he said, "Pete. Where were you when Jack was being robbed?"

MapHead swallowed. "I was here. I came home."

"Leave him alone. It wasn't his fault," Jack said smartly.

"You came home." Jack's father's eyes locked with MapHead's. "Yes," he said, after a moment. "You study at home. I see."

The rest of the evening's viewing slipped away uneasily. Supper was cheese straws and cocoa. MapHead politely declined a sausage roll. He didn't eat animal protein these days, not ever, unless he *had* to. He drank his cocoa cold. Then he ate twenty cheese straws, one after another, like a train. Then he went into the kitchen and ate some Wegbiscuit. Wegbiscuit came in a packet that said PACKED WITH CALCIUM—BEST FOR YOUR DOG. The hexagonal biscuits were pink and pale green and pretty hard to snack off if anyone else was around. Up on the roof again after, Jack said, "Could you do that for me?"

"Do what?" MapHead opened his book.

"That thing you did with my dad. Making him think what you want him to. I mean, could you make 'em think what I want 'em to? Like,

I'm, you know—make Dad like me a lot?"

"He likes you already."

"You think?"

Jack had his geography homework, Map-Head the *Wonderworld of Knowledge* he'd been reading earlier in Jack's room. Leafing to *Penguins, Emperor,* he chocked himself comfortably into the V between the chimney and the roof and took up where he'd left off.

For a while MapHead drank in facts quietly. First the female emperors laid their eggs. Then they passed them over to their mates and went to sea. Then the Antarctic gales closed in, and the emperor dads sat them out. It was hard to believe what he was reading, except he'd seen it himself—the huddle that few men had ever seen—a mass of thousands of male emperor penguins shuffling around like little old men in cardigans so they each faced the wind in turn, in temperatures cold enough to crack beaks. And they stood there for up to two months. With eggs on their feet. In darkness. Without any food.

It was incredible how they did it. Many froze or starved. Those that didn't, did it all over again next breeding season. On it went, and on—and no one knew they were doing it. No one knew to this day—MapHead read— no one knew to this day how many emperor penguins there were, nor how many emperor penguin huddles, because no one knew how to count 'em. The only reason they could huddle at all was, they were in it together. Shared heat. Fitting in. Each of them one among hundreds. And every single one of them had their dad.

They have to hand 'em over in ten seconds, see? he sent Jack Stamp.

"Who?" Jack picked up the thought without thinking.

"The dads," MapHead said. "Once the chick hatches, the dad keeps it warm in his pouch. When the mums finally come back the dads have to hand over the chicks in *ten seconds or less,* else they freeze to death while they're doing it. The chicks I mean, not the fathers."

"We're talking penguins here, right?"

"Right. Baby-sitting for two or three months with nothing to eat in the freezing cold wind in the dark. King of Dads, or what?"

Jack shrugged. "King of Baby-Sitters, I guess."

MapHead flashed up a map. *I'm thinking about Cape Crozier. That's where the first huddle anyone ever saw was. Know what it was near?*

"Surprise me."

"Scott's hut. Mr. Scott who went to the South Pole and never made it back?"

"You should come into school," Jack said darkly. "You'd do Rickers's head in, you would."

"Rickers?"

"Mr. Rickman. Year eight geography. You come into class, right, do Argentina all over your face, see Rickers do his loaf."

"His loaf?"

"His nut. Do his head in." Jack sighed. "Go mad."

"Right." MapHead nodded. Mad he understood. "Want some help with your geography? Anything you want, I can map it."

"Nah. What I'm doing about homework is—" Gripping his exercise book between thumb and forefinger like a shoe that had stepped in something, Jack held two terms' geography work, up to and including Shales and Demographic Displacement, at arm's length. Then he dropped it down the chimney. "What I'm doing about homework is, I'm winging it."

"Don't do that. It's a *book*." MapHead was scandalized.

"Right," Jack said, "a *dead* book."

Shales and Displacement, Igneous Interludes, plus Marshland Regeneration fluttered away like dead birds in the soot-smelling mouth of the chimney. Jack brought out physics with Mr. Wiseman. Math with Mr. Rains. Chemistry with Miss Preston. French and German with Brownsie. One by one, Jack Stamp posted his entire stock of year eight schoolbooks down a blocked-up chimney no one used. The books, Jack knew, would back up into a fusty heap behind the blocked-up fireplace in the dining room downstairs. No one would ever find 'em. Else he wouldn't have done it.

"What did you do that for?" MapHead watched, aghast. Hugging the *Wonderworld of Knowledge,* he flashed up an anxious little map of the Zuider Zee. "What did you do that for? How will you do schoolwork now?"

"I won't." Jack grinned. "I'm quitting."

"But you can't just stop going to school."

"Why not? You can do anything you want, and I can't?"

"You can do anything, but—I don't know— you have to *choose.*"

"I can choose, all right," Jack said. "I choose life over brain death, freedom over school."

"Sometimes it isn't," MapHead said, desperately.

"Isn't what?"

"Freedom. Sometimes it isn't what you thought it was when you wanted it to start with. When you can do anything you want, *choosing's* not so easy."

"*Choosing.*" Jack mimicked MapHead. "Choosing what?"

"The right thing to do."

Jack shrugged. "Nothing I do makes a difference."

"*Everything* you do makes a difference." MapHead held Jack's eyes until Jack dropped them.

Long after Jack Bradley Stamp had gone to bed, MapHead sat drinking in the nightscape. Growing tips of plants made a crisscross grid of energy, stretching way off to the moon. Way off, the sewage farm hummed. A bird buzzed by. A fox called. The green-winking night ticked and glowed. MapHead cast his eyes around. Nothing in the world escaped him. MapHead had eyes for everything.

Frosted in flooding moonlight at the highest point of the roof, MapHead stood alone in an attitude of power. Beneath the slates beneath his feet, the family Stamp slept fitfully. He threw back his head and arched his back. The object of power was smooth in his hand.

With both hands MapHead raised the smooth, meshed dish—the dish that messed up the telly, so mysteriously lodged on the roof, almost, it seemed, just for him—and ran his thoughts around it and with it made a point of desire. The point of desire would attract whatever he wanted. It would poke up in the soupy stuff of the Subtle World like a raised toe under the sheets. And when it did, something would happen.

I need you, Dad, MapHead sent out like a pulsar, without much hope of an answer. Hadn't his father told him he must solve his own problems, sink or swim? Probably Powers wouldn't come, no matter how hard he—MapHead—pleaded. But maybe he would help.

Help wore many disguises. MapHead dreamed he met Powers that night in a fiery place, subtly real. They walked through curiously textured landscapes together. Powers burned like a brand. MapHead held out his arm. Livid spots ran over it. He wanted more than anything to brush away those spots. *I don't like them, Dad. Help me brush them off.*

You put them there yourself. Only you can brush them away. His father held his eyes and questioned, always questioned. *Are you doing the right thing? Can you be sure, my Map-Head?*

9

FEAR OF A KIDS' PLANET

"Pete! I forgot to ask you! Can you swim?"

"'Course I can! Don't worry!" MapHead waved back to Valerie Stamp across a swimming pool filled with heads and shoulders. Then he walked up to the deep end with the heat and the noise pressing down on him like ten atmospheres of Jupiter.

The swimming pool was loud and bright and filled with turquoise water and many-voiced echoes that flung themselves into the roofspace and stayed there, booming and hooting. Children dressed in not very much yelled and shrieked and swam into irritable adults. Others popped, surprisingly, out of a green pipe the shape of an intestine. MapHead watched intently. A girl in black-and-white stripes climbed a spiraling staircase over the pool and disappeared at the top. After a while the same girl popped out of the green intestine, rather more surprised than she'd started. Map-Head grinned. It really was a funny thing to watch. He couldn't have imagined, when swimming pools were mentioned, that this— this *intestine* place—would be what Jack's mother had in mind. Pools, MapHead knew, were generally green and rock strewn. He must have heard it wrong. This must be a swimming *flume*. Meadowpark Sports Center. FLUME OPEN TEN TO TWELVE-THIRTY. That, at least, was what it had said outside.

The noise and confusion were incredible. The changing room—for changing your clothes, not your mind, Jack's mother had carefully explained—had been bright and hot and noisy. So noisy, it had filled MapHead with a longing for wide, open spaces with any-thing soft underfoot. Jack had lent him a pair of blue shorts for swimming—Jack called them trunks, nothing to do with elephants—and warned him three times *no maps,* but things had not gone entirely smoothly. Already Map-Head had locked his clothes in a locker and lost the key, mainly because he'd panicked when required to wear it on an orange rubber band around his wrist. He felt hot and on edge and pretty near a life-threatening tantrum.

If it hadn't been for the water, MapHead might yet have run away.

The wonderful water waited. Crystal blue and curiously chemical smelling, the deep end had signs saying DEPTH 2 METERS and other signs saying NO BACK FLIPS, NO BOMBING, NO SPITTING, NO SPLASHING, NO SNORKELS. PLEASE. MapHead peered worriedly down, afraid he might do some, or all, of the things on the sign, should he once get a foot in the pool. He cautiously dipped in a toe. The water was warm and used feeling. Wavering red lane lines marked its bright blue depths. MapHead slid gratefully in. He didn't wave to Jack, racing Saturday morning mates under the clock. He didn't wave to Holly, floating, amazed, in her bright yellow seated plastic ring. Instead he sank coolly to the bottom, tasting the water as he went. Chlorine was present in an alarming amount. No need to worry. Cool and blue would do. Through the wavering water on top of him, MapHead watched the hot red lines of a chair on extra-long legs with a man in blue on the top of it. There were several men in blue, MapHead had noticed; one by the green intestine, one on the long-legged chair, one who walked around and around, blowing a whistle now and then. They had MEADOWPARK CENTER in gold on their shirts. They didn't go in the pool at all. Maybe they couldn't swim.

After he'd been six and a half minutes on the bottom, MapHead turned lazily over. Divers plunged over him with sleek hair and bodies, trailing streams of bright bubbles from their mouths. Children exploded into the water sensationally under the intestine. A forest of interestingly shaped legs waggled and jumped in the shallow end. MapHead closed his eyes and felt better already. The pool had cleared his head to no end. It made an entertaining spot to relax for an hour or so.

All at once the tone seemed to alter. Map-Head opened his eyes. The waggling legs were standing to attention. A whistle blew. Voices belled over the water. A face appeared and stared down at him, hair fanning around its goggle-eyed edges. MapHead tried to sense what the trouble was. Something—what?— had gone wrong. Maybe a man in blue had fallen in the pool, after all. *Deep panic vibrations overhead.*

Suddenly a spear of white bubbles lanced into the water. As MapHead watched wonderingly, it turned into a musclebound man in blue trunks. The man in blue trunks kicked down to him purposefully. MapHead's heart jumped up. A man in blue trunks was swimming down to get him. What had he done?

Was it bombing, spitting, or snorkels? He hadn't meant to. He didn't know. All, or none, of these?

The man in blue trunks dived right down and seized MapHead forcefully under the arms without even asking if he minded. He kicked with him back to the surface. Map-Head fought all the way. He tried to go back to the cool turquoise depths he'd been dragged from, but the musclebound man was stronger and determined to have his own way. Thoroughly panicked and outraged, MapHead fought more on the surface, grabbing anything he could get hold of to get away. Somehow the long-legged red chair got involved. So did the man with the whistle. So did Valerie Stamp.

The struggle involving three lifeguards, the lifeguards' red chair, and the manager took quite a long time to sort out, and the sparkling turquoise pool was pretty much spoiled for MapHead in the end. It wasn't that they weren't understanding, it was just that he felt so hot and cross. Drowning. Of course he hadn't been drowning. He had, MapHead insisted, only been *resting* on the bottom. Couldn't they *see* he was fine?

"Don't worry, it wasn't your fault." Jack's mother parked the car and smiled. "Home at last. I expect these things happen all the time."

"They do to *him*," Jack said. "They don't to anyone else."

MapHead took Holly indoors and put on the kettle for tea. Jack hung towels and swim-suits out, grumbling as he did it. Mrs. Stamp answered the phone. She twirled the phone flex around and around her finger, listening, nodding, understanding. MapHead pricked up his ears.

"What about Pete Burns? He's a treasure. He can do anything with the baby. Holly adores him. Yes. Looks a bit strange, I know, but—of course he does, yes, don't worry. *Really* good for a baby-sit."

Valerie Stamp beckoned to MapHead over the phone.

"Lois? Lois can't do it. On a Saturday night, are you kidding? Yes, but Pete Burns can. Give him a go. You'll like him."

She gave a thumbs up to MapHead. Map-Head grinned, he didn't know why.

"Seven-thirty okay? I'm sure he would. I'll send him over. Are you swimming next week? We've just been to Meadowpark. Not really, no. Boundary Road Baths is better. See you there Tuesday? Great. Okay. Got to go." Valerie Stamp replaced the phone. "Well," she said, "that was nice, wasn't it?"

"Can we go swimming again?" MapHead asked. "I won't do any more resting."

"Not the Meadowpark Center again, I don't think." Mrs. Stamp winced, remembering the scene. "But swimming somewhere, of course. Meanwhile, how about a job?"

"A job?"

"Seven-thirty tonight. My friend Tanya needs a baby-sitter at short notice. I told her you were good."

"I am, aren't I?" MapHead was thoughtful. "She might think I'm funny looking."

"I told her that."

"Oh."

"She knows it's fine if I say it's all right. She'll make it two-fifty an hour. Unless, of course, you'd rather not?"

Valerie Stamp looked anxious and drawn, MapHead thought. Probably on account of Jack. Jack being beaten in had really upset her a lot. Plus, he was being a pain. Jagged, edgy, demanding things, breaking things, slamming out of the house, not—MapHead couldn't let on—not really going to school much more than the odd day here or there, "to stop Rickers going ballistic," Jack's act couldn't go on, yet it couldn't seem to stop. MapHead tried not to worry. Worrying didn't help at all.

"I can easily say you can't do it. Would you like me to say you can't do it?"

MapHead threw Valerie Stamp a smile that widened to include all her problems, all his, and most of the world's. It doesn't, said Map-Head's smile, it doesn't really matter *at this moment*.

It's fine. The smile widened. *Don't worry. Be happy.*

Valerie Stamp looked at MapHead. "You know, Pete, we'll miss you when you go. Especially with Jack's acting up." Tears welled in her eyes. "I don't understand what's made him like this. I really wish it would stop."

MapHead's heart did a double flip. "It—I mean, he—will. Stop, I mean, I'm sure."

"I hope so. He's not a bad person."

"How much did Jack weigh?" MapHead asked, after a moment.

"When he was born? Eight pounds, ten ounces, exactly."

"Heavier than Holly."

"Yes, I suppose he was."

"Maybe you should tell him sometime."

"I think he knows."

"He'd like to hear it," MapHead said sagely. "Trust me. I know about these things."

Valerie Stamp wiped her eyes on her sleeve. Pete Burns had such a funny take on things.

She smiled half crossly through tears. She couldn't help herself.

"Anyway," she said, "it's twenty-nine Rhames Terrace."

"What is?"

"Tanya's house. Jack can show you this evening."

MapHead nodded. "Fine." Then he went to find Jack.

After lunch Jack's mother finished the dishes still smiling over Pete Burns, thinking what an extraordinary person he was, how he always made her feel better, how magic his touch was with the baby. If only Jack could be more like him. Jack was the only trouble.

Then she made a cup of tea, thanking her stars the kitchen was straight as she did it. No need to look for the biscuits in the muesli bin anymore. It had taken a while, but at last things were back as they were. Good thing whatever had happened—what *had* happened?—wasn't likely to occur again since she'd fixed up a visit to the doctor. It's all down to stress, the doctor had said. Take things slowly. No need to worry about it. Plenty of people moved things and couldn't remember they'd done it. Valerie Stamp bustled around for tea bags. As soon as she opened the cupboard over the kettle, *Pete Burns's Seafood Kitchen* jumped out and hit her smartly over the head.

She picked up the book and looked at it. What an extraordinary person Pete Burns was. How extraordinary he should have the same name as—as this cookery book in the cupboard. Valerie Stamp sat down. She felt subtly different since the knock on the head. Cogs in her mind long silenced started to turn over slowly. A flood of questions welled up.

How much did she really know about Pete Burns, anyway? How long would his parents be away in Greece? Why couldn't she picture his parents? Remember how she'd offered to put him up while they were away? Any arrangements that were made?

Valerie Stamp looked into her tea. Maybe she'd forgotten it all. These days, she couldn't be sure of anything. She got up and looked down the corridor to see Pete Burns, plainly eavesdropping, flattened against the wall outside the living-room door. She withdrew quickly, heart thumping. Pete Burns was really quite strange. She would have to have it out with Jack. Who was Pete Burns, really? What was he in their home *for*?

"I need decks and a mixer." Jack Stamp stood

over his father. "I need some decks, like, *now*."

"Decks?"

"And a mixer. Like, I need them *yesterday,* all right?"

MapHead flattened himself against the wall outside the living-room door. These voices had business together. Business that didn't need him. MapHead applied his eye to the slit where the door met its frame. Through the slit he could make out an armchair and two figures, one sitting, one standing. Mr. Stamp and Jack. Father and son. Not so much together, as on different sides of a wall. That's what it seemed like, at least. Alan Stamp looked up over his paper.

"No, it's not all right. What d'you mean — decks?"

"Twin turntables. For mixing. Techno, hardcore, hip-hop."

"Like a disco setup? For music?"

"That's the one."

"What for?"

"I want to be a DJ—so can you front me something for it?"

"Front you something for it?"

"Can you lend me the money for a deposit?"

A week or two had gone by since Jack had come home bloody, days in which Jack's mood had darkened. He'd not seen MapHead much. MapHead baby-sat, Jack brooded—in various depressing places, sometimes in school, sometimes not, mainly up the multi, despite what had gone down before. He needed cash *big time* now, Jack had tried to explain to MapHead. Especially since he got ripped off for the Valet Packing take. But MapHead didn't like money. He wouldn't go Valet Packing. Money didn't eat, he knew already. What he'd learned with Jack was that as well as having no appetite, it had no conscience. MapHead didn't—wouldn't—listen to Jack about money. Neither would his father.

"I don't want to hear it, Jack."

"Just *listen* a minute—"

"How much are these things, anyway?"

"Ben Pringle's brother's selling his."

"How much does he want for it?"

"Them. A hundred and fifty, maybe two."

"Is that all?" Jack's father lowered his paper. "Look, I know you've had a rough time lately, but this isn't the way out of it, all right? I still don't understand what you were *doing* on the estate."

"I told you. I went to see Starkers."

"But Martin Starkey lives on Smucker's Row."

"It was the Smucker's Row end of the estate."

"You're sure about that, are you? You don't seem very sure about anything else that happened to you."

"I'm sure."

"And you didn't recognize the boy who hit you?"

"I told you. No, I didn't."

Greenslades Estate—not the multi—so far as the Stamps were aware, the scene of their son's assault, hadn't recommended itself to MapHead on first acquaintance. He'd visited it once or twice with Jack. But he hadn't liked it very much. Greenslades had the same air of cold and neglect as the multi, like nobody cared very much what happened to it—or them—while they were there.

"Well, next time don't hang about." Alan Stamp returned to his paper. But Jack wasn't about to give up.

"He'll take a deposit."

"Who will?"

"Ben Pringle's brother. That's why I'm asking. So can I have something up front?"

"Can you have something up front? How about a kick in the pants?"

"I'm serious. How can I be a DJ without any decks?"

"I'll deck you myself in a minute. Give it a rest."

"Up the Revolution." Jack looked down on his parent with naked hate in his eye. "Fear of a Kids' Planet. One Nation Under a Grouch."

Jack swept icily out. Jack's father thought a moment. Then he folded his paper and shouted after Jack, "*What was that you said?*"

Jack paused at the front door. There were other rap titles he could've pressed into use for insults, but none his father would understand, so there wasn't really much point. MapHead followed Jack out of the house, more than a little puzzled by what he had to do. For one thing, he had to calm Jack. Jack was well out of order. It wasn't what he wanted to *do,* so much as the full-on way he wanted to do it. DJ BlackJack, New Name of Outrage, was one cool dude—when he wasn't blowing the lid off the whole of his life to date. He had a family and a dad to himself. Wasn't that enough?

"Hey," he told Jack, "don't puff it."

"Puff it?"

"Blow it, I mean."

"MapHead, leave me alone."

"My name's Pete Burns, if you mind or if you *don't* mind."

Jack Stamp and Pete Burns crossed the street together at the crossing—a pelican crossing, Jack said—more than a little aggro with each other. First Pete Burns had wanted to know why there weren't any pelicans. Then he'd wanted to wait for the green man to light up. With a clear road either way, Jack Stamp had grown impatient.

"You don't *have* to wait for the green man, all right?"

"Why's the green man *there,* then?"

"He's just, like, *extra,* okay? You're really teeing me off. Mary fussing Poppins, or *what*?"

MapHead pricked up his ears. The Poppins woman again. Clearly an expert on road safety as well as safety at heights, she certainly put herself about. He pictured a strapping woman hung about with ropes and picks and flashlights. Then he added a lollipop stick and a hat. It made a strange sort of image, not entirely friendly. MapHead mentally filed it. If he could find out more about the Poppins woman, there was a chance he could flesh it out later.

"I'm baby-sitting Saturday," he told Jack as they walked on.

"It's Saturday today."

"It's seven-thirty. Tonight. And you're supposed to show me where it is."

"Is that right?"

MapHead nodded. "So will you?"

"I've got better things to do," Jack said grimly.

"Like what?

"Like Big Shout 2."

MapHead felt his pulse race. "When will you do him?"

"Now."

Jack turned in at the multi. With his stomach lifting like it was about to show him his breakfast again, MapHead turned in after him. Immediately the growl and stink of maneuvering cars made MapHead's nostrils contract. Scorning the stairway, Jack marched straight up the concrete ramp to the heart of Level B. The concrete ramp led them steeply up clockwise with the kind of defensive twist a castle stairway might have so that no one could draw his sword on his right-hand side. With its passages and levels, its echoing stairwells and elevator shafts, its painted nooks and chambers, the multi wasn't so different, MapHead supposed, from a kind of medieval castle. A castle and a kingdom, for those lonely enough to soldier it.

Jack Stamp was all eyes and vengeance. Rapidly he scouted Level B. Then he signaled to MapHead across an orange-lit crypt of car-tops, *Nothing—you?*

Nothing, MapHead signaled back, sweating at every pore.

"On up," Jack said, rejoining MapHead with a hawk-eyed military air. "Level C. Let's go get him if he's there."

"Let's not. Let's do Nuns and Tadpoles instead." MapHead pulled Jack's sleeve really quite hard as they went. "Can't we do fishing in that nuns' pond? Like we did the other day?"

"No," Jack said, "we can't. I'm not doing Nuns and Tadpoles. Nuns and Tadpoles is stupid."

"Let's go up the estate. Go and see Starkers, can't we?"

"Stuff Starkers." Jack shrugged his arm free. "This is serious. He's got my key, you know?"

"Who?"

"Who do you think?"

"Big Shout 2 has your door key?"

"That's what I said. He stole it, remember?"

"I don't think we ought to do this." Map-Head blocked Jimmy-Jack bodily. "I think we ought to go home."

Jimmy-Jack coldly sidestepped. "So go home if you want to."

MapHead gripped Jack's mind with his. *We should stick together always. Remember what you said?*

"So?" Jack stared. "What did I say?"

You and me together. We don't need anyone else.

"Yeah, well," Jack said, "that was then." But he wouldn't meet MapHead's eyes.

"I could stop you," MapHead said. "I *could* get inside your mind and make you want to go home, except you're free to do what you want."

"I'm free," Jack said, "that's right." And walked away.

10

THE BABY-SITTER

MapHead felt bad all afternoon. Supposing Big Shout 2 were six—or seven—feet tall? Supposing Big Shout 2 beat Jack up, and he— MapHead—wasn't there to help him *again*? But Jack was free. He had to *choose,* and he'd chosen.

Pretty soon MapHead spotted Lois. It wasn't too hard, in a high street of shops fizzing with Saturday shoppers. Lois went shopping every Saturday. There weren't a million other things to do. At about the same time MapHead spotted Lois, Lois spotted him back. Off she went in a gaggle of friends and pretended she hadn't, but her laugh took on a self-conscious note all the same. MapHead followed as if attached by a string to Lois's back, deftly dodging strollers and ladies in too-tight dresses.

Lois flounced as she walked. She looked, MapHead thought, kind of *fluffy*. Lovely, fluffy long hair flounced and bounced behind her and her shirt fanned out beneath it as she walked. MapHead followed Lois and her friends through Top Look, where they all browsed dresses and disappeared for quite a long time into the changing rooms and came out again more or less the same as they went in, only pinker; through Crystal Cauldron Candles, where they smelled every essential oil in the place and came out really quite fragrant; through Boots, where he watched them try on makeup until the woman on the checkout, who'd been staring hard at him for some time, made a move to approach him around the counter. MapHead bolted next door into Woollies, where he waited under Irish sphagnum moss peats, heart thumping, in the garden accessories section.

Soon Lois and her satellites drifted by like the center of the universe. MapHead slipped after them into Smiths. Smiths was bright and many colored, flagged with magazines and posters and cards and stands with a multitude of books. First MapHead looked at the pencils. Every kind of pencil was represented, from childish thick red crayons to steely refillable stilettos. He spent a while with spiral binders and document wallets. What were all these things *for?*

Suddenly Lois rounded the stand. She looked kind of *confrontational,* MapHead thought.

He put on a smile for her anyway. "Hi, Lois. I'm doing shopping."

Lois's eyes snapped. "Are you following me?"

"I'm looking at pencils. Why would I?"

"Yeah, right. Coincidence you're *here,* like you haven't been in every other shop I've been in."

MapHead eyed Lois sadly. "You don't like me, do you?"

"I don't *not* like you. I don't think about you either way, all right? So stay away if you don't mind."

"I really don't, if you—"

"And you can *stop* following me around all the shops."

Lois marched off to look at magazines. MapHead wandered sadly into books. *Teach Yourself Italian* failed to shed much light on whatever it was he'd done—*was* doing— wrong. Pretty soon he had to look at Lois. Lois's warning to stay away went around and around in his head. Did she mind him so very much? She'd bothered to come and tell him so.

It seemed as though she did. MapHead wasn't the only one to think about Lois's warning. Lois turned once to see what the effect had been, just as MapHead turned to show her he didn't bear a grudge and wasn't about to follow her anymore. Their eyes met over Junior Fiction.

A peculiar moment passed.

You think I haven't been watching you? Lois's eyes held MapHead's. *You think you can just arrive out of nowhere and live in someone's house when they don't even want you and be totally weird and creepy and they're just, like, going to* accept *you?*

MapHead opened his mouth, then closed it again. He would've given a lot to look like a bookstand. He didn't have to read Lois's thoughts. Her eyes spoke clear across the shop: *Mum's changed. Jack's changed. You think you can make me think what you want?* Lois's eyes widened. *I know it's down to you. What are you going to do about it—change me as well?*

MapHead flashed up a big loose map over his head. Then he backed away. The map pulsed over his scalp, crazing his face with rivers. A space around him widened as people turned to stare. MapHead tried to smile, but the loose map ran on the smile and made it lunatic and blue around the edges. A stand that said CLASSICS AT BEDTIME: GEORGE ELIOT, MRS. GASKELL, JANE AUSTEN fell down with a clatter behind him. MapHead slid around on the shiny slick covers of *Emma* and *The Mill on the Floss* while alarm bells sounded all over, both inside his head and out, before gathering himself and running out. The bright lights hurt him. Lois's eyes hurt him. The names on the stands, the colors, the shapes, the books themselves, the people staring after him hurt him most intensely.

MapHead ran and ran. He ran past the Co-op, he ran past Spar, he ran past Do-It-All. He didn't stop running until the Nuns' Pond. Sinking gratefully into the murky, tadpole-speckled water deep in the flower-flagged terraces where the nunnery brooded on Jack's street, MapHead let out a long string of bubbles and allowed his sense of self to dissolve like an Alka-Seltzer.

Sister Wilhelmina noticed a ripple. Parting the curtains in the refectory overlooking the garden, she said, "I thought I saw a fish jump. Quite a big one, too. My word. Did you see that fish?"

Precisely an hour later, MapHead sat up. Unlooping a long string of pond weed from around his neck, he got up and went into town refreshed. Then he remembered who he was. Then he remembered who else knew who he was—or suspected, at least, there was more to Pete Burns than met the eye. MapHead sighed. She'd never really trusted him. Lois was going to be a problem.

"Hey, Jack! Jack, wait!" It wasn't any coincidence MapHead met Jack leaving the multi. MapHead had a *subtle* sense of timing. Jack didn't look too subtle. In fact, he looked kind of shifty. Plus he was running full out.

Oweeee — oweeee — oweeee — oweeee — oweeee!

The air vibrated with the sound of a car alarm, way up in the blaring multi. The sound beat down on Jack and MapHead and everyone else looking up or running away. MapHead felt vaguely panicked. He kept up with Jack with an effort.

"Is it thunderstorms? Why are we running?"

"No one asked *you* to. Bog off."

"Don't say that. You hurt me."

"Aah. I hurt him. Wibble."

"Jack! Wait! *Wibble?*"

"Yeah. Wibble. Feel sorry for yourself, why don't you?" Finally Jack slowed a little. He looked MapHead up and down. "Why are you soaking wet?"

"I did Nuns and Tadpoles."

"Oh."

"What about you? Did you find him?"

"Who?"

"You know. Big Shout 2."

"Oh. Yeah. It's sorted."

"Did you get your key back?"

"He's bringing it. Next time."

"So is he big?"

"Massive. Almost did me in."

Jack ducked into Home Street. That was what MapHead called it, on account of its being the street with Jack's home in it. Really the street was named Gough Street, but Map-Head thought Gough Street sounded like a noise you made in your throat. Way up in the tall trees cresting Gough Street the nunnery brooded with its pond. MapHead inched a slug of pondslime out of his sleeve. Exactly the place he'd come from, he was heading back toward. Funny how things went in circles. Except when they went in crossed lines, like the wires between him and Jack.

"So how did you pay him back?" he asked Jack quietly. "Big Shout 2, I mean."

Jack looked mysterious. "I got ways."

MapHead looked solemn. "He must've had a horrible life to want to hit people."

"That doesn't make it right."

"It gives it a *reason.*"

"Maybe he's all mixed up. Maybe he doesn't know why."

Jack dashed an arm across his face. He seemed mixed up himself. MapHead tuned in, but Jack was blocking him out. They walked on in silence, threading the roads home in the half dusk with the car alarm fading behind them and Saturday afternoon dying on the streets in thickening shadows pooling into one another to make up a still early evening. No one said anything much. There was nothing much to be said.

Teatime passed uneventfully. The only thing MapHead noticed was that Valerie Stamp seemed edgy. She looked at him in a funny way. She spoke a little coldly.

"Pete. I don't seem to have a note of it. When do your parents get back?"

MapHead looked at Jack. Then he looked at Lois. Lois raised an eyebrow. She got up and pushed in her chair. "I have to call Stiggy. Thanks for tea."

Mrs. Stamp frowned. "Do you have to call him *now?*"

"I do if I want to go out."

Lois left the room. Soon they heard her voice on the phone.

"Eight-thirty? Can't you make it nine? Okay. Mandeville's. Maybe."

"So, Pete." Valerie Stamp returned to Map-Head. "When did your parents say?"

"They said," MapHead said carefully, "they might not be back for a year."

"A *year*?" Mr. Stamp looked up.

"To Greece," MapHead amended hurriedly. "They said they might not go back to Greece for a year. Because of having such a good time now."

"So when are they coming back *here*?" Alan Stamp gave MapHead his full attention. A pulse in MapHead's head began to jump. He looked at Jack for help.

"Here? About—" MapHead considered the ceiling, as though choosing his words with care. "Oh, about—"

"About seven-thirty, isn't it?" Jack Stamp checked his watch. "I thought Pete was baby-sitting. Won't that make him late?"

"Oh, no." Valerie Stamp covered her mouth. "Tanya's presentation dinner. That stupid clock. Of course it's not ten past four."

"I'll take him round now if you like," Jack offered. "Might stay and keep him company."

"I wish you would." Valerie Stamp looked at Pete Burns. Why had she recommended him to her friend? Tanya would think he was strange, mainly because he *was* strange. Too late to stop him now. But better with Jack than

134

without him. "I wish you'd baby-sit together," she finished. "That way you won't get bored."

Jack and MapHead got up and went out hurriedly. But Valerie Stamp called them back.

"Pete. Before you go. Have I a number for your mother?"

"A number. No."

Valerie Stamp waited. "Well, can you give me one?"

MapHead smiled glassily. "Oh. Yes." Then he made up a number. "It's eight hundred thousand and two. And a half."

"I mean a telephone number. That doesn't sound right."

"800-0002," translated Jack. "Plus the code for Greece."

On the way to 29 Rhames Terrace, Jack said, "That was close. It's wearing off. You'll have to fix her up."

Well off fixing people up, MapHead nodded miserably. Things were getting complicated, the way they always seemed to if he hung around for a while. The traveling life stayed footloose and free. Footloose and free and lonely. Soon he would have to—he supposed—move on. But first he would baby-sit for Tanya. He could be the best baby-sitter Tanya ever had. A baby-sitter she would never forget. And Jack would be there to help him.

135

MapHead put his best foot forward. On the steps of 29 Rhames Terrace he set his chin and put on—what he hoped was—a sparkling smile.

Jack Stamp looked at MapHead. "Two-way split, right? How much are you getting?"

"Um, two-fifty an hour."

"We'll say we thought it was three. That way it's one-fifty each."

Jack Stamp knocked smartly at the door. Then he stepped back and waited. MapHead waited too, improving his smile, so that it was quite fixed and taut when the door opened.

"Good grief. Are you the baby-sitter?"

Tanya Rhodes opened the door on Map-Head's grimace. The grimace took her aback. She'd been warned he'd be funny looking. But this kid looked like an apple.

"Sorry we're late, our clock stopped," Jack explained. "This is Pete Burns. Mum said to come together."

"Thanks for coming at short notice, Jack." Tanya considered MapHead. "So this is Pete Burns. You'd better come in, I've got to get my skates on."

MapHead smelled Tanya's heavenly scent on entering. Her eyes, her dress, her hair were heavenly, too. He watched her shrug on a coat. Where were the skates she'd mentioned? He wondered why she needed skates—wheels on feet, not fish—when she looked so perfect already. MapHead took in the vision that was Tanya done up to the nines. He really was quite bowled over.

So, it seemed, was his charge. The small boy in pajamas in front of the telly had turned to stare at MapHead like his neck was permanently stuck.

"Must dash. There's Coke in the fridge and sausage-flavor Krackles on the side," Tanya told them. "Maxie goes up at eight o'clock. I said he could stay down till then."

The small boy in pajamas rushed across to his mother. He clung to her, wailing thinly. "Iss him," he wailed, "that funny boy. *An' I want to come with you.*"

"Now, Maxie." Tanya frowned and detached him. But Maxie wailed and wailed.

"Give him a drink," Tanya advised. "He'll settle down soon as I've gone."

As soon as she'd gone, Maxie settled. Only minutes after the front door had closed on his mother, Maximillian Rhodes was running a space probe, experimentally, into Jack Stamp's feet. Jack Stamp turned up the telly. He put up his feet and flicked through the channels. Then he said, "Maxie. Get me the Coke 'n' Krackles."

Maximillian Rhodes buttoned his lip and looked at MapHead. He turned on his heel and fetched the Krackles. Then he sat down on the farthest possible edge of the settee away from MapHead and stared at him fixedly.

MapHead smiled. "I thought you'd be a baby. But you're not."

Maxie edged farther away. His mother might've forgotten the boy in the bubble of light in the multi-story car-park one Tuesday at SuperFare, not so very long ago.

But Maxie hadn't forgotten.

11

MAKEOVER

"Okay, Maxie. Bedtime."

"I don't want to." Maxie twisted away from Jack's hand and continued his game on the floor. It was the kind of game that crept under your skin and stayed there, involving as it did the frequent collision of Tonka trucks with the leg of Jack's armchair.

"Hey, Maxie. What did I say?"

"And-this-one's-coming-back-little-bit-too-fast-zaz-zaz-zaz-urrrch! Tip-alla-stuff-up, oh no, it fell out! Captain's coming! Got to—urrch-urrch-zaz-zaz-ZAZ-an-off-he-goes-again—"

"MAXIE! BED!" Jack looked fierce.

"Nogunna." Maxie set his chin defiantly.

"Nog-unna?"

"Not going to," MapHead translated. "I don't think he wants to go to bed."

Jack plumped into his chair in disgust. He flipped a few channels. "Well, when then?"

"When what?"

"So when *is* he going to bed?"

MapHead inclined his head as Maxie's truck negotiated the top edge of the settee and launched itself, rocketlike, across the fatal gap toward the armchair. "ZAZ-ZAZ-ZAZ."

Jack wrenched the truck off Maxie and put it down coldly beside him. He coldly pushed the nose of Maxie's teddy with his foot. "Take that thing away, will you? I don't like the way it's staring at me."

Maxie considered Jack calmly. With icy dignity he turned to revisit his toy box in the corner. For a moment everyone forgot about Maxie. A re-run of the first episode of *Beverly Hills 90210* washed smoothly over Jack and MapHead. MapHead helped himself to a banana from the fruit bowl. Then he ate another. And a third. They were nice, but— somehow bananas didn't quite hit the spot.

"BEE-BAH, BEE-BAH, BEE-BAH"— materializing with enormous violence and a realistic-looking fire engine with siren and flashing blue light, Maxie jumped up in Jack's ear. "BEE-BAH—EMERGENCY 911— FIRE! FIRE! LOOK OUT!"

Jack leaped up like his chair was on fire.

Maxie—wisely, as it happened—bee-bah'd on out to the kitchen. "BEE-BAH BEE-BAH, FIRE ENGINES COMIN'"—

"That's it," Jack said. "I'm killing him."

"As baby-sitters we have to preserve him," MapHead said worriedly.

"What did you think, I'm really going to kill him?" Jack looked at MapHead. "Of course I'm not going to kill him."

"I knew that." MapHead tried a smile. He didn't know what to think.

Maxie brummed back in. They watched him negotiate the furniture with a futuristic-looking rocket in fluorescent plastic and chrome. The rocket made a noise like a cross between television interference and someone with very bad phlegm. Also it had a laser gun. The laser gun made a noise like an electric gorilla coughing inside a video arcade. Jack watched telly fiercely. He looked, MapHead thought, a little tense. Jack was usually tense lately. Also, his mood changed a lot. Oblivious to its danger, Maxie's Intastella Explorer laser-gunned its way around the room. The angle of its trajectory from Planet Kitchen to touchdown brought it perilously close to an orbit around Jack Stamp.

"Can't you shut him down?" Jack turned up

the telly. The combined noise sounded like a gorilla going mad in a gun shop.

"What d'you mean, shut him down?"

"Well. You could make him go to sleep if you wanted, couldn't you?"

"I suppose I could, if I—"

"Do it."

Something ticked inside MapHead's head. Hadn't he been here before? Wasn't there a point—or something—at stake?

"He's driving me nuts." Jack glared. "You can make him think he's tired."

"Yes, but—"

"So make him think he's tired."

"No." MapHead rose angrily. "I won't. You didn't want me in *your* mind. Now you want me in his?"

"He's just a kid. This is different."

"No," MapHead said, "it's the same. *And I'm not interfering in anyone's mind anymore.*"

MapHead stormed out to the kitchen and looked in the fridge. He searched around impatiently. There was some dietary itch he needed to scratch. Margarine. Cheese. Milk. None of them were *it*. The food looked kind of gray and old and tired. Especially the cheese. The cheese was going moldy. Map-Head felt strangely angry with everything and

everyone in view. There was so much Jack
didn't understand. Maybe he should tell him.
MapHead slammed up the fridge and stormed
back in to Jack.

"Anyway," he told the back of Jack's head,
"it's not so easy, doing these things. There's
only so much around."

"Only so much what around?"

"Energy. In the Subtle World. It's all con-
nected, see? What happens here, happens there."

"I don't understand what you're talking
about."

"Where I come from—the Subtle World—
see, it's only the other side of this one."

"What are you on?" Jack dimmed the
volume on *90210* and finally gave MapHead
his attention. Maxie had melted away. "The
other side of *what*?"

"It's like "—MapHead took a deep breath—
"it's like another dimension, sort of. Invisible,
but *around*. Side by side with everything, you
know, ordinary."

"Invisible but around. Another dimension.
Right."

Jack turned back to the television. On
screen a guy in a black leather jacket spilled
out his pockets onto the police department
desk. A cop in blue suspenders picked up a
book of matches. Close up, a name and

number revealed the address of the Blue Hawaii Motel.

"You don't see many kids like me," Map-Head continued sadly. "Less energy, see? What goes around, comes around. Maybe I'm one of the last."

Jack stared.

"That's why I like babies. They're like, beginnings we don't have?"

Jack stared some more. The on-screen cop behind his head moved quickly to seal off the bank.

"There *are* others like me. Like my dad, I mean, at least." MapHead smiled uncertainly. "Did you think there weren't?"

"I don't know. I didn't think anything." Jack's mouth felt numb.

"And things aren't so good anymore. That's why they're coming in."

"Coming in where?"

"All over. You see 'em sometimes, in the sky."

The feeling that he was on the brink of something huge grew upon Jack with every passing moment. What *was* it about Map-Head? Undreamed-of possibilities seemed just within his—Jack's—reach. All he had to do was open his mind.

"I feel like my head's bursting." Jack's

breathing came shallow, then shallower. "I
know about star clusters. I know about spatial
displacement in four dimensions. I know how
to fix a baby's diaper three different ways. I
know about *ancient Rome*. I know, like, mil-
lions of things I never knew before, and I
haven't got *room* for them all."

"What's the chemical composition of a
cat?" MapHead tested gravely.

"Ninety-eight percent water, two percent
carbon compounds, plus calcium, minerals,
trace elements. Nutritional content: fifty-eight
percent useable protein. How did I know
that?" Jack held his head. "*I know too much
and I want it all to stop.*"

"It's my fault," MapHead said sadly. "I
swapped your pictures for mine."

"You swapped my pictures? How do you
mean?"

"Mainly memories," MapHead explained.
"I wanted to show you everything. I wanted
you to *understand*."

"Understand what?"

"How I want to fit in." MapHead hung his
head. "It seemed like a good idea at the time.
Go ahead, if you hate me."

"You interfered." Jack's eyes glowed. "*I
want my own pictures back.*"

"You will, and I'm going to fix it." An

enormously sympathetic map of southern Australia lit up MapHead's head. He got up to reassure Jack. "Soon as I can, I'm fixing it. I never meant it to change things."

Jack sidestepped MapHead, his mind already on other things. "Watch out, will you, I can't see the telly."

"The thing is, I don't know what's wrong. I didn't know this would happen."

"This what?"

"You. Being weird."

"Me? Weird? And you're not?" Jack switched telly channels. "*Mad Max* rerun. Cool."

"I'll fix it so it's okay. I didn't mean to do it and I *promise*."

"Promise me another Coke, if you're going out to the kitchen." Jack waved MapHead out of the way. He draped himself over his chair. "Give yourself one too, if you get that kid in bed—where is he, anyway?"

MapHead's map subsided. He watched Jack watching telly. Unable to concentrate on anything for more than a minute or two, Jack was seriously strange. Hadn't anything he'd said meant anything at all?

Wandering back out into the kitchen, less angry this time, MapHead's attention was held by the large and imperious-looking plant on the windowsill. *Cyclamen*, his mind whispered. *Bulbous. Winter flowering. Can be forced on throughout summer.* Immediately attracted by its juicy stems and imperial purple flowers standing up straight like butterfly wings, MapHead took a bite. Then he took another and another, finally holding the wide-bottomed plastic pot in both hands and scything across the plant with an open mouth. MapHead closed his eyes and chomped on a mouthful of stems. This was it. Brain food. The trace elements he'd been lacking fell into place like the tumblers in a lock.

It was while he was finishing up that he noticed Maxie under the table. Maxie stood up slowly. Hurriedly replacing what was left of Maxie's mother's houseplant, swallowing down stems as he did it, MapHead turned to face Maxie. There was a long—a very long—silence.

Finally Maxie said, "You were angry, weren't you?"

"Just now?" MapHead nodded. "I was angry."

"You've got no hair."

"No." MapHead smiled. "I haven't."

"Would you like some?"

"I suppose."

"You're funny, you are."

"Yes," MapHead said, "I'm funny."

MapHead brushed away a suspicion of stem from his mouth. It said a lot for Maximillian Rhodes's composure that he didn't run off and hide. Most people didn't eat houseplants, MapHead realized. Especially not in that ravenous, scything sort of way. Most people would probably have run off and never come back. But Maxie hadn't. Plus, he had something to say. MapHead waited. Maxie would spit it out in his own good time. In the meantime, he couldn't honestly say he regretted the cyclamen. The cyclamen had really hit the spot.

"When I was in the car-park"—Maxie edged a little closer—"when I was in the car-park, I saw you in the light."

"You saw me in the light." The boy in the car in the multi—how many weeks ago now? MapHead looked at Maxie. How much could Maxie understand? "I waved to you, did you see?"

Maxie nodded a lot more than he needed to. Then he nodded some more.

"That's the way I travel from place to place," MapHead explained. "The light takes me where I want to go."

"Is it hot?"

"No, it's not hot."

"Did it make your hair fall out?"

"That's right. It falls out every time."

"You better not do it then. Maybe you'd have some hair."

"Maybe"—MapHead said, enjoying himself now—"maybe I would."

A longish pause followed.

"'F you want hair"—Maxie held up a felt-tip pen—"'f you want hair, I can do it."

MapHead considered Maxie. "Do I have a choice?"

First Maxie drew on mustaches. Then he carefully colored MapHead's scalp in running lines of broad-tip dark brown paint-stick. He made a careful parting. How about burners? Could he do burners? What are burners? Map-Head asked. Soon he knew, because he had them. It seemed they were bits of beards. Side-beards, down from his ears. Soon Maxie wanted to join them under his chin. But Map-Head drew the line at a beard right down his neck.

MapHead wanted a mirror, but Maxie grew standoffish. Not yet. It wasn't finished, all right? Maxie raced upstairs and returned with a silk-finish zip-up that smelled the same as Tanya. Tipping it out onto the settee, he picked out a flat pad of powder and patted it over Map-Head's face. MapHead picked out a tube or two from the jumble on the settee. Most said

COVER LIPS MOISTURE PLUS. One or two said things like CINNAMON CRUSH or PINK TWIST or GINGER UP, as well. Others said EYES HAVE IT, MOONSTRUCK BLUE—disconcertingly, Map-Head thought.

It turned out Moonstruck Blue was exactly the shade Maxie had in mind for MapHead's eyebrows. After the eyebrows he had a bright idea. Racing upstairs for a scarf and a hat, Maxie finally displayed the finished effect to MapHead in front of the mirror.

MapHead stared back at himself. He was forced to admit Maxie had made a difference. He looked like an eccentric forties' film star forced to cover up due to some frightful disease of the skin. Maxie held up a plastic case. He forgot the false eyelashes. Where were they, anyway? MapHead covered his mouth. He'd only eaten one.

Jack said, "You look stupid. What d'you let him do that for?"

"He's tired," said MapHead. "Look at him."

"Look at *you*, you mean."

MapHead put Maxie to bed, meekly, in his own little darkened bedroom replete with a glowworm night-light. He kissed him and closed the door. Then he opened it again.

"'Night," said Maxie, the top of his head just visible beside his ted's.

"'Night."

"Pete." Maxie called MapHead back.

"What?"

"Nothing. You look really funny."

MapHead grinned. "Wonder why?"

"Will you come again?"

"Maybe. I don't know."

"In the car-park, maybe? In the light?"

"In the light," said MapHead. "Good night, Maximillian Rhodes."

"'Night, Pete Burns. G'bye."

Good-bye. MapHead stood uncertainly outside the door. What should he reply? Should he lie and say, "See ya soon"? In the end he stood silently, choked, for a long time. Then he went downstairs again with a totally satisfying warm feeling halfway between pain and tenderness burning inside his chest. He drank a liter of milk to damp it down a bit. Then he put his decorated head around the living-room door.

"I'm having a bath. Wash this stuff off."

Jack grunted. "Good job, 'cos I'm not being seen out with you till you do."

With his arms folded in front of the telly Jack looked, MapHead thought, quite a lot like his father.

Tanya got in at eleven-fifteen with very bright eyes and a collapsing hairstyle. She expressed her surprise that Pete Burns and Jack had had no trouble with Maxie. Usually Maxie played up. The dinner? *Really* good. Steak in peppercorns, and sorbet. Plus she won Ferrero Rocher in the raffle. Talk about whacked. She'd call Jack's dad to pick them up. Thanks a million, how much did she owe them?

Soon after they got in and climbed the darkened stairs to bed, MapHead rose off his supposed bunk in Jack's room and lay down at Holly's bedside and went instantly to sleep with no trace of guile or guilt about him. Maxie would be sleeping deeply, too. It was a job well done. MapHead smiled in his sleep, curled like a hedgehog on the floor. He'd made, he thought in his dreams, a *proper* baby-sitter. Better'n the Poppins woman, any day.

"Mappers. You awake? It's me."

"What?" MapHead looked up groggily. Jack's face loomed above him. "What is it? Don't wake Holly."

"Why are you always in here?" Jack asked, bug-eyed in the light from the landing.

"I don't know. I like it. What's the matter?"

"Nothing. Only—I wondered."

"Like me to come in with you?"

Jack nodded manfully. "Yeah, I really would. I sort of felt—frightened, you know?"

"Frightened of what?"

"Being alone."

"Alone is scary. I know what you mean."

"Plus, I'm scared of myself."

"You're scared of *yourself*?"

Jack nodded. "All these things I'm thinking. And I saw a ghost, you know? Behind the bathroom door."

Back in the attic room under the stars, Map-Head watched Jack sleeping. His open door said JACK'S ROOM, ALL RIGHT? If only it really were. Poor Jimmy-Jack Stamp knew too much, yet too little, and none of it was his fault. His own part in Jack's dilemma hit MapHead between the eyes. He would have to set it straight, and soon. How was another matter.

Long before morning ruddied the sky, Map-Head had decided. The hollow place in the runner beans, where he'd sat and thought long and hard, was hours since cold and abandoned. The morning light shone in at a certain bedroom, through a certain denim blue blind. It shone on Jack Stamp's bed, it shone on Jack Stamp's books and clothes, it shone on all the sticky bits in Jack Stamp's bedroom carpet. It shone most especially on Jack Stamp and the freshly painted message on the wall beside his bed. Jack Stamp opened his eyes. The smell of spray paint hung in the air. Letters sprayed in spray paint marched beside his bed. Jack Stamp sat up. The wall beside his bed read:

JACK—
Gone 2 find Dad. Gard Holly 4 me.
Catch U later. Pete.

Gone to find Dad. Catch you later. Pete. Where in two worlds had the oddball with the agitated scalp taken off to so suddenly? Map-Head, gone? Where? Jack held his head. He ground his teeth. He buried his face in his pillow. He writhed and rolled in bed. Finally he flipped up the blind. A day without Map-Head flooded in. A day without friends or purpose.

12

WIBBLE

"Dad! Dad! Where are you? I need to know what to do!"

Through all four dimensions and all through a whole Subtle World, MapHead searched for his father. His father watched him do it. He curled his lip and wondered, When will he ever learn?

"Dad! I know I'm not meant to. But I need you to tell me. Please, Dad! I mean it. Can you only tell me what to do!"

It was a little painful for Powers to listen to his son bleating in all four corners of the globe. Painful, but unfortunately necessary. He launched away in space, as MapHead got too close. His son had almost caught him in South America. Only the dusty summit of hill-fort Machu Picchu had gotten in the way. It had *been a close shave, too, at the pyramids. Lucky King Cheops had built in a place to hide. And the misty mountains of Mourne had posed a problem or two. At the misty mountains of Mourne, MapHead had been close on his trail. At his son's approach, Powers had flashed away to the Giant's Causeway on the northernmost coast of Ireland. The Giant's Causeway surprised him. A layer cake of odd-shaped rocks tilting out to sea, it looked, Powers thought, like the scene of some wild party. Someone—giants—had partied wildly and left behind their giant cake topped with shattered candles. Powers sat down to wait. Presently his questing son glowed among the candles.*

"Dad! Are you there? Is that you?"

Powers sighed and flashed away. There would come a point when he'd take a hand in MapHead's affairs. Until then every appeal, every cry for help or advice must fall on stony ears. His son had come of age. He must solve his own problems, sink or swim. That was the point of leaving him, no matter how urgent his cries. Even the one that followed him, faintly, on the wind:

"Dad, wait, don't go! I did this thing I never meant to! Now I know what you meant and I'll never, ever—Dad! I know you can hear me! Wait for me, Dad—are you there?"

• • •

MapHead took a deep breath and sat down heavily on a rock. The Spartan sea rocked in a basin before him. The Spartan hills, with Spartan valleys under them, looked down. Cypresses stood cool and tall and gracefully spaced, wherever the sky needed lancing. Wherever it didn't, rounded clouds of olive groves rolled away into the distance.

MapHead sighed. He was going to stop somewhere. With its tranquil light and brilliant blue bays, Greece was as good a place as any. As good a place as any without a father or a conscience he could live with, which no amount of *traveling* would discover. He would never find his father. Not while his father didn't want him to. Instead, he must find something else. Self-respect, for starters. It wasn't fair that he should have to do everything without any help. It wasn't fair that he was always alone — why *was* he? He only had all the power in the world, yet here he was lost on a hillock, somewhere in Spartan Greece. Aah. Poor MapHead. *Wibble.*

Feeling a bit sniffy and more than a little sorry for himself, MapHead walked alone along the shore. Silvery fishes darted as one in needle-bright shoals when he feinted throwing them food. They even sucked his toes, for want

157

of anything tastier. MapHead looked up. The brilliant sun beat down on the Spartan hills. Sparta, home of the brave.

MapHead knew about Sparta. It had something to do with leaving babies on hillsides to die and sending young boys away to nasty-looking camps with not enough clothes or food, and they musn't complain. And they combed their hair before battle, and their mothers had rather they came home dead on their shields than come home ashamed. Spartan boys stole what they could or they went without. It was a point of pride not to get caught. They wore a thin shift no matter how bitter the weather and never said, "Mum, where's my sweater?" or, "Chilly today, don't you think?" They slept on hard pallets and washed in cold water and—probably—dried themselves on bushes or something else prickly. They probably sharpened knives on their thighs. Probably they rolled on thorns or opened sores for fun. MapHead looked out on the china blue bay. Here the Spartans had raided fisherfolk and robbed them of conger and octopus. They didn't farm or fish themselves, why would they? Wherever they went, they simply took whatever they wanted. Strength. Courage. No regrets. No matter what happened, they wouldn't complain. The Spartans had to be the most wibble-less people on earth.

And the Pass of Thermopylae. At the Pass of Thermopylae, Spartan King Leonidas had held off King Darius's *whole Persian army* with only three hundred men. Way to go, thought MapHead, reaching the broad promenade. Here the little seaside town traded its fish with tourists. MapHead, a tourist in more ways than one, felt he should do some shopping. Plus, he felt peckish at last. Following the smell of bread just out of the oven, MapHead entered a stooped little shop with not much more than a smile to pay his way.

The baker looked up. *"Kalimera."*

MapHead swallowed. It was all Greek to him. Maybe the baker said, "Good day." Maybe he said, "Get knotted." It didn't really matter much. Nothing MapHead said to him back was going to make much difference.

MapHead held the baker's eyes. He pointed, slowly, deliberately, one after another, to a golden loaf topped with sesame seeds, triangle-shaped pastries gleaming with something very sticky indeed, and an amber pot of honey with a picture of bees in clover. The baker handed them over one by one, not looking, his eyes firmly locked on MapHead's.

"Thanks a lot." MapHead smiled. Then he said, slowly, deliberately, "You've done enough.

You should retire and go fishing with Eric. Eric wants you to."

Then he let the baker go. Baker Stoupos scratched his head. He watched the boy with the bread and honey leave his shop and trail away up the hill out of town. Then he took off his apron. The sky and the sea were a lazy afternoon blue. Tonight he would take the boat out with a bright light to draw octopus. He would stand in the bow with a spear and jab out their brains. His friend Eric Christos was right. He should fish while the fishing was good. It was time he retired and enjoyed himself. Hadn't he worked all his life?

The smell of oleander and hibiscus followed MapHead as he climbed the village road to the hills. Beside a vivid field of poppies he passed the village school. The children tumbled out and made their way home for siesta, chattering noisily—very much, MapHead saw, like children anywhere else. They didn't notice the poppies or the oleander, the swooning hibiscus, or the cheeses hanging to dry under flower-laden verandas. These were things they passed every day, why would they notice them now? Plotting and unplotting the surrounding hills and coastline over his increasingly active scalp, MapHead climbed sweltering foothills through hot sage and wild oats, pausing only once or twice to look down on the dwindling blue bowl of the bay.

Way up in the Spartan hills, long after the bread and the pastries were gone and the honey all dripped, luxuriously, into his mouth, MapHead fell in with a man dressed all in purple. At least, the man was very far ahead when MapHead heard a yelp. Reaching a beautiful garden, MapHead saw a fox. A little fox with bewitching yellow eyes and deep-fat puppy fur. The fox cub yipped. MapHead's pulse beat fast. Then he remembered Spartan boys took whatever they wanted and died before they got caught. Reaching over the fence into the beautiful garden to tickle the fox pup where fox pups most needed tickling, MapHead weighed its weight in his hand. He wanted it, no question.

By the time he reached the man dressed all in purple, the fox cub was safe in his shirt. More than a little wild and scratchy, he thought—he hoped—it would quieten down in time. The man in purple turned as Map-Head drew smartly abreast. His mouth widened and smiled under sea blue eyes, saying something, anything, friendly.

Kalimera, MapHead returned. The fox cub stirred in his shirt.

"I said, are you going far?" The man in purple repeated.

MapHead had the feeling that the man had spoken in Greek. But strangely, his greeting made sense.

"Far as I need to. Not really."

"What do you mean, not really?"

"I'm not really going anywhere. I don't have anywhere to go." MapHead heard the self-pitying note in his own voice with something like surprise. Did he really feel so hard done by?

"It is better to travel than to arrive," the purple sage advised.

"I hate that." MapHead sighed. "That's what my father says."

"Better, by far, to find your own way than to have someone else choose it for you—don't you think?"

MapHead scanned the road ahead for a fast way to lose the man in purple. He didn't feel like a lecture. Plus, the fox cub was murder. Squirming and wriggling under his shirt, the fox cub meant to escape. For something so cute and appealing—*ow!*—it felt pretty vicious close up.

"Who knows what decisions we may have to make, what we might have to do?" the purple sage was saying. "These hills, this path—that next turning up ahead. Who knows what—or who—may lie around it?"

"May lie around it," MapHead echoed, his attention anywhere but on the man in imperial purple. He'd have thrown down the wriggling fox cub then, except that Spartan boys *didn't get caught*. They'd both passed the beautiful garden. If he threw down the fox cub now, the man dressed all in purple would know that he was a thief. A thief, as well as someone who played with people's minds, then didn't know how to set it straight. MapHead felt like crying. He held the fox cub tightly under his shirt. Wasn't he in Sparta, now? He mustn't— *wouldn't*—complain.

"I'm sorry," MapHead continued, "but I've been on my own a long time. I don't know what to talk about when I bump into other people."

"Talk about yourself," the purple sage invited. "What better thing is there to talk about?"

"About a million better things," MapHead answered darkly. "I'm not so great that I want to *talk* about anything I've done."

The man in imperial purple stopped. "What *have* you done?" he asked MapHead.

The blue Spartan sea swam behind the sage's gaze. His sea blue eyes questioned

MapHead. MapHead swallowed. Was it *that* obvious? Did he wear his guilty feelings all over him like livid spots he couldn't brush off, not even—especially—in dreams? Did they swim on his face like contour lines? Did they ring like a leper's bell? The matter of answering the man in purple honestly and *not dropping the fox cub* had become as thoroughly entangled in MapHead's mind as Jack Stamp and wrongs unrighted.

"What have I done?" MapHead took a deep breath. "I only messed up my friend's mind, plus the whole rest of his *life,* plus the whole rest of his *family.* Then I ran off and left him, just when he needed me most."

The purple sage inclined his head. "And?"

"And what makes it worse is, my dad told me not to. Interfere, I mean. So now I want to put it right, but I don't know what to do."

"So you knew it was wrong when you did it?"

MapHead opened his shirt. He took out the fox cub lovingly. The fox cub regarded him with golden yellow eyes with a pinprick of black in the middle. It tried to wriggle down through his fist. Its pink mouth tried to bite him.

"So you knew it was wrong when you did it?"

MapHead set down the fox cub. It scampered lightly away. MapHead watched its silly little brush tail flickering away through the dry grass under the olives. *Power is responsibility. Don't take advantage. Respect.*

"Yes," he said with a full heart, "I knew it was wrong when I did it. And I'm," he added, "the only one who can fix it. And that's just the way that it is."

It hurt him so much to say it. MapHead held the feeling close and knew it for a friend. Some things were good for you, like medicine. The fox in the beautiful garden — the purple sage, the china blue bay, the dream of Spartan Greece — were things in the order of these. He hadn't complained, after all. He'd faced up to himself like a hero. Wibble-less at last, he was free to act as he chose.

Flushed with triumph after all, MapHead glowed on the path. The last thing he remembered was the hot smell of sun-dried grasses, bright with butterflies, murmurous with honeybees. Then something broke inside his head, and Spartan Greece flashed away.

13

NO LOVE NO HOME THIS SUMMER

The dog Weg looked at the digger. MapHead looked through Weg's mind's eye. It was a long time—had he ever?—it was a long time since he'd tried to see things from a dog's point of view. The digger roared, churning up mud as it lifted a log with its bucket-that-opened-in-the-middle. The bucket-that-opened-in-the-middle swiveled. Then it set down the log, gingerly, on the topmost tip of two other logs, balanced one on top of another.

The scene was a strange one to start with. Through a dog's eyes—through Weg's eyes, at least—it made no sense at all. As if it weren't all confusing enough, when he'd looked around after materializing as close to Jack Stamp as he was able, MapHead had had a job working out *where he was at all,* never mind at some kind of show. At Rubytown & District Agricultural Show, as it turned out. At the Digger Competition, to be precise.

The Digger Competition seemed to involve enormous earthmoving machines with limbs like crabs moving tiny objects in impossibly delicate situations. After the competition to set one log, end up, on top of another without toppling them, the diggers moved on to a line of empty bottles. MapHead watched incredulously as a digger driver picked up a single bottle with his crab-claws. The excavator's huge serrated claws, as big as a dinosaur's jawbone, held that bottle as lightly as an egg. Hugely straining and roaring, the digger set the bottle on a plank. Then it went back for another.

After MapHead had witnessed competitor Dean Wellcome's digger levering itself over a pole with much crunching of gears and insect-like maneuvering of arms and struts and buckets, he still didn't understand it. The dog Weg didn't understand it either, MapHead could see. Jack Stamp and his family understood it, but waited to see what would happen. It was good to see Jack and his family again. Wasn't that Martin Starkey, as well? MapHead dodged their eyes. He would join them when he was ready.

"And Dean Wellcome . . . going well now against the clock," droned the loudspeaker. "Three bottles in position . . . lovely job, Dean . . . and going on now to tackle the Floating Balls in the Skip . . ."

Fruity smells wafted into MapHead's brain as the dog Weg sniffed its way into the Rare Breeds and Ewes Enclosure. MapHead checked the family Stamp. Surely they'd notice their dog had wandered off? Apparently not. Totally involved in Dean Wellcome's bid to skim balls out of a water-filled skip with the business end of his digger, no one seemed to have noticed the Wegster's move. MapHead wrinkled his nose. Then he followed Weg, seeing what Weg saw, smelling what Weg smelled. And was there ever plenty to smell in Rare Breeds and Highland Ewes.

Odor-radiating sheep of every size and texture eyed MapHead fearfully over the tops of their pens. Black-face sheep, white-face sheep, Jacob's Sheep, rugged moorland crossbreeds, and sculpted-looking show queens with flat backs the width of Welsh dressers—such a bewildering mass of heaving, lanolin-smelling bodies brought MapHead up short in his tracks. All of them were sheep. And all of them were smelly. Smellier than anything MapHead had ever sniffed before, they weren't at all unpleasant. In fact they smelled quite—exciting.

Wagging with joy from head to tail, the dog Weg sneezed three times. MapHead sneezed three times in sympathy. With a sense of smell so sensitive a million whiffs a second swamped your brain like a funfair you could sniff but couldn't ride, pulling you this way, then that, filling your head with a hundred edible scents, the sheep tent was Sniff-It Heaven. The dog Weg thought so, too. No one noticed Weggie Wegsford approaching an aisle of ewes. He wandered between them, sniffing. MapHead searched the ewes' minds. He probed their syrup-colored eyes. Nothing. Worse than Weg. Just *nothing* but fluff. And fear.

"Get that dog out! Now!"

A large agricultural type, with a red face and a white coat with bursting buttons so tense they'd explode any minute, bore down on Weg. MapHead sidestepped to avoid him. Then he sidestepped again.

"Don't dance with me, boy. *Get that dog out!*"

Bursting out of Rare Breeds and Highland Ewes hot on the heels of Weg, MapHead turned a corner, then another, finally dodging down a miry passage ankle deep in straw behind a barn. Weg ran on, but MapHead didn't. Instead, he stared at the boy. A boy with a spray can. Spraying big marching letters on a concrete-block wall. The concrete-block wall of the barn.

"And Frank Doidge bringing years of experience to bear on these balls in the skip now . . . ," boomed the loudspeaker, somewhere beyond the sheep tent. "Going on now to Stack the Can . . . and Dean Wellcome building up an impressive lead in this event. It's going to take some beating. . . . Is Frank Doidge the man to do it?"

"I went in the sheep tent. I just got chased out." MapHead smiled uncertainly. "It's pretty smelly in there."

"So surprise me." The boy spraying paint on the wall was really pretty skinny.

"What are you doing?" MapHead asked.

"What's it look like? Tags."

"Tags?"

"Tag lines. IDs. Riffs, you know?" The boy continued spraying. He didn't miss a beat.

"But why are you?" MapHead persisted.

"Why am I what?"

"Why are you writing it on the wall? Why don't you write it on a piece of paper or on a computer or something?"

"I dunno. Because." Finally the artist looked at MapHead. "Why did old Leonardo de Thingy paint pictures? Why didn't he just doodle on bits of paper?"

"He did," MapHead said simply. "He did lots 'n' lots of doodles, all the time." *Leonardo Da Vinci, 1452–1519,* MapHead scanned in his mind. Then he added, "I could show you where he lived, if you like or don't like."

The artist stared. "*Don't* like."

MapHead controlled his scalp with difficulty. Probably plotting a map of the small Tuscan town of Vinci would be too much, anyway. Way too much, at this stage. Better not come on too strong. Not with some kid he just met.

Still looking at MapHead, the artist shook his spray can. Then he turned away and finished spraying

No love no home this summer
Big Shout 2

"*You're* Big Shout 2?" MapHead boggled.

The artist sprayed on. "No prizes."

"You're not very big. Can you shout?"

"It's my tag line, all right?"

"Do you live here?" MapHead felt muddled. Was *this* the robber who beat up Jack Bradley Stamp?

"Oh, yeah. I'd live in a field."

MapHead weighed the tone of this reply.

No love no home this summer. Then he said, "So where, then?"

"Where what?"

"So where do you live?"

"Over on Greenslades. What's it to you?"

"So you *do* have a home."

"Foster home. My mother, she don't want me."

A blast from a distant-sounding horn announced the end of the sheep-shearing contest. The *neee-yaw* of the Rotary Saw Display chewing through half a tree trunk sounded peevishly over the *pom-pom-pom, tiddle-om-pom-pom* of the silver band playing the Flora Dance. Over the top of the hedge MapHead spotted Jack; then Mr. Stamp, dragging Wegsy, disgraced, on a leash; then Mrs. Stamp, with Holly, all trooping back to the car.

MapHead looked down. Then he said, "Those shoes. They belong to my friend."

"Says who?"

"I say. Me. 'Cos they do."

"Yeah, well." Big Shout 2 considered his feet. "Yeah, well, he owed me. Your *friend* put one over on me. Till my brother showed up."

"He did? I mean, Jack, he—did something?"

"Only robbed me blind."

"Jack was robbing you? And then your brother hit him?"

Big Shout 2 wiped his mouth. "Rob—that's my brother—Rob got my money back off of him. Plus we got all his. Then Rob smacked him a bit. Then he ran off and fell over."

"He lost his door key as well."

"Rob's got his door key. You better watch out. My brother, he—does things."

"What things?"

"Houses, mainly. Sometimes cars. Whatever he feels like doing."

"I do things too," MapHead said helpfully. "Mostly maps. Plus, I'm living with this family and trying to fit in? We're over on Gough Street. You should drop in sometime."

"Maybe we will." Big Shout 2 smiled crookedly. "Rob likes dropping in."

"Is that why he's called Rob?" MapHead went on pleasantly, "Because he robs things?"

Big Shout 2 stared hard at MapHead. "Who are you, anyway?"

"MapHead," said MapHead. "Look. I can do tag lines too."

First MapHead tagged Verona. Then he tagged Ravenna and Bologna. Finally, the whole of northern Italy. Crisp in every twist of river, lake, and bluff, the map was a physical map and one of MapHead's best.

The graffiti artist blanched. He capped his spray can robotically. "I'm out of here," he said.

MapHead watched him back away, fast, then faster, so eager to go he'd go any way he could, no matter how much mud from behind the barn he took with him. It was funny what maps could make people do. It was funny what people did, anyway. It was funny—or tragic—the things that they wrote. A few words could say so much. When nothing of Big Shout 2 remained but his jumping tag line on the wall, MapHead finally emerged from behind the barn. *No love no home this summer.* A purposeful smile lit his face.

Jumping up onto the wall, MapHead looked down on Rubytown. A family town to Map-Head: the place his own mother and half brother and grandmother lived and worked and ate their meals and went to school and dried their hair and drank tea and broke their nails on supermarket blister packs, and watched their favorite soaps in. Home, with all that that meant. It gave him an idea. Suddenly filling his lungs, MapHead shouted with all his might:

"Dad! I know what to do! You don't have to tell me anymore! I know what to do about Jack!"

Jack Stamp. Where was he? Popping out

anxiously into the car-park field below, Map-Head spotted a line of departing cars in time to see the Stamp-mobile joining it. The Volvo looked so familiar by now it felt like a toe or an ear. MapHead could make out Jack Stamp's head behind his parents'. Beside him, Holly's car seat. On the other side of that, the well-disgraced and tousled head of the hound they called Weggie Wegsford. Jack wasn't looking back. But there was something about the back of Jack's head that made MapHead want to join him very much.

Vaulting a gate into the road ahead of the Stamps' departing car, MapHead stuck out his thumb, the way he'd seen hitchhikers do it. The slow-moving line of cars rolled past him unhurriedly. No one stopped when they saw MapHead's thumb. Maybe they hadn't seen it. A sign saying HEAVY PLANT CROSSING worried him more than a little. He scouted the road. No heavy plants. Then he spotted the Volvo. He waved his thumb and waited. The Stamps pulled up obediently.

"Which way are you going?" MapHead inquired politely. He needed a cardboard sign, he knew. One that said ALL ROADS HOME.

"There you are, Pete Burns." Mr. Stamp wound down his window. "We wondered where you'd gone."

"Where I'd gone." MapHead found Jack's eyes. Jack's eyes ate him up.

"I said we'd meet at the show," Jack improvised. "I told them you'd gone with Dave Wilkie."

"Dave Wilkie?"

"Dave Wilkie you went to have lunch with," Jack said, meaningfully.

"Oh." MapHead blinked. "Dave *Wilkie*. Right. I really like Dave Wilkie. 'Specially lunch with Dave Wilkie, then we meet at the show. And I say I've known him a long time. And what I like is, to meet him. Mainly for lunch and a show. Then I say I've — "

"Pete." Alan Stamp checked the line in his mirror. "Would you like to get into the car?"

Squeezing in between Jack and Holly's car seat, MapHead noted that Lois was absent with disappointment tinged with relief. He met Valerie Stamp's gaze inches from her face. Valerie Stamp smiled at him rather uncertainly. Then she faced front over a large bargain begonia with tasty-looking leaves. She exchanged a look with Jack's father. Then she turned back to MapHead. "Could we talk later, Pete? There's a few things we'd like to ask you."

"Talk. Later. I'd like to." MapHead squirmed. *Very* much later, he hoped.

Jack almost wept with relief. Except he kept it well hidden. First he pinched MapHead so hard he almost yelped, but didn't. Then the whispering began.

"Mappers. Where have you *been?*"

"Once round the pyramids. Twice round the Giant's Causeway. Plus I went to Sparta."

"Seriously."

"Seriously. How long have I been gone?"

"Last night," Jack said, "and today. Feels like a million years."

"A million years in *subtle* time. And anyway. You missed me."

"Not you," Jack said, "the maps."

"Just the maps?"

"I'm joking." Jack Stamp bit his lip. "I thought you'd never come back."

"As if," MapHead told him, holding Jack's eyes, letting Jack see where he'd been—if he wanted to, that was. *Pyramids. Sea fog. A hill fort in South America. The candle cake at the Causeway. A china blue bay. An olive grove. The prickly hills of Sparta.*

"Oh," Jack said, "I see."

"What's that, Jack?" asked Mrs. Stamp. "What did you say you see?"

"Nothing. I said, time for tea."

"Can you wake Holly? We're almost home. Teatime it certainly is."

MapHead shook Holly gently as Mr. Stamp killed the engine on Gough Street. Holly's blue eyes opened, misted, focused. Her pink face puckered irritably. MapHead scooped her out of her car seat before she could start to cry. Holly examined MapHead's chin. She smiled in MapHead's eyes and smacked him on the head. MapHead smiled back. Holly liked him. She let him know. It felt good to know she missed him. Jack had missed him, too. It felt warm and right inside to reclaim his place beside them. It felt like fitting in.

"Hungry, Pete?" asked Mrs. Stamp. "I'll bet you could eat a horse."

"No thanks," said Pete Burns seriously. "Egg and chips is fine."

14

THE BLACK HOLE

Hubert Sewell Community College
Outlands Road
Rubytown
Tel: 01533 396876

May 16, 1996

Mr. and Mrs. A. S. Stamp
Rising Sun
Gough Street
Rubytown

Dear Mr. and Mrs. Stamp,

You will recall that I wrote to you recently in connection with Jack's erratic attendance at school, suggesting a meeting might be in order and proposing a possible date for you to come in. I'm sure you will be as anxious as we are to discuss any problems Jack may be experiencing. I will be available next week any day except Wednesday from 3:30 onward. If you would care to phone my secretary to make an appointment I will look forward to seeing you then.

Yours sincerely,

Ada Leary

Ada Leary
Headteacher

Ada Leary. Headteacher. MapHead rolled the name around on his tongue. It was a name he'd heard Jack mention often enough. Ada Leary. Makes you weary. Plus, she used to be a man. Supposedly. MapHead had heard all about it. Someone had said it once, for a joke. Now fantastical stories abounded, supported by anything as slight as an uneven bust line or an extra nasal hair. Poor Ada Leary. At any rate, she didn't sound too cross—or manly—in her letter. More worried than cross. But *how* worried? How long would Ada Leary smolder before she blew?

Hearing Jack thump up the stairs, Map-Head hastily folded the letter back into its stiff-looking envelope stamped with the Hubert Sewell Community College logo and slipped it under the carpet with the others. He'd learned to spot them a mile off, once he'd learned about letters. The first time the letters came through the door when MapHead—and no one else—was up, MapHead had blocked their passage through the letterbox and forced them all back out. In they'd come again. Map-Head pushed them out. A tussle of kinds had developed between the postman and Map-Head. The postman had gotten quite angry. Finally MapHead had opened the door and accepted the crushed-looking letters after the postman pointed out they were addressed to— and wanted to be received by—the people named on the front. Ever since then there'd been a truce between MapHead and the postman. The postman's name was Crispin. Map- Head tried not to mind.

MapHead had recognized the letters from school as a threat the moment he'd seen them. Jack would be right soon enough. No need to discuss any problems. Even so, he couldn't hold it forever. The situation re: Jack had elements of coming to the boil. The threatened talk with Valerie Stamp hadn't materialized yet. Once or twice over the week since his return she'd looked as if she was up for it, but greeted with MapHead's candid gaze had somehow always backed off. Instead, she'd grown peevish with Jack. Jack couldn't do anything right. Hyperactive and as cutting as acid in any reply to his mother, Jack didn't help himself. He looked pretty normal, but was he? What was normal, anyway? Just what had Jack been like before he'd known him? MapHead couldn't afford to dwell on it. It would undermine his certainties. Certain hard-won certainties were just about all he had.

Jack put his head around the door. "So."
"So."

"What are you doing?" Jack joined Map-Head on the spare bed, MapHead's bed, in his—Jack's—bedroom.

"Nothing. Just looking around."

"Want to look at my brochures?" Jack meant his travel brochures. Following a visit to Hoseason Travel in Fore Street, Jack had spent a lot of time, of late, poring over pictures of white beaches and extravagant purple sunsets. Sri Lanka, Island Paradise. Discover Turkey. Aloha, Hawaii! Romantic Granada. Exotic Algeria. Unforgettable Algarve. Sun-kissed Canaries. Getaway Caribbean! Jack Stamp had read them all.

"Why don't you read things you're meant to?" MapHead asked.

"I'm not going to school, if that's what you mean."

"Something's going to happen if you don't."

"I've been in, now and then. What more do they want?"

Jack shoveled his brochures back under his bed. Then he looked at MapHead.

"You won't go away again, will you?"

"Of course I'll go away."

Jack swallowed. "But you'll come back. Every time. Won't you."

MapHead smiled. Jack even *sounded* like him, these days. "I came back the other time,

182

didn't I? Nothing ever really goes away."

"'Cept your dad. You said you never found him."

"I don't think he wants me to find him."

"You want your dad, I want mine," Jack said, simply.

"You've got yours already."

Jack raised his eyebrows. "Have I?"

MapHead considered Jack Stamp. Jack Bradley Stamp had had enough on his plate just lately without thinking his father didn't like him. Behind Jack's head his—Map-Head's—funny marching letters still vaguely announced his departure. GONE 2 FIND DAD. GARD HOLLY 4 ME. Poor Jack Stamp. The scrubbed-out message on his bedroom wall was one more reason he was grounded.

"How do you feel?" MapHead asked Jack.

"Bored out of my mind. How would *you* feel if you knew what I know?"

"I *do* know what you know. Plus I know loads more as well."

"Well, then. You know how I feel."

"You know Big Shout 2," MapHead started. "I saw him the other day. You know you said he was massive—"

"He isn't, his brother is." Jack's eyes snapped. "I pushed *him,* his massive great brother pushed *me,* and I lost my door key, all right? It doesn't matter now, anyway. We're past all that. On higher ground, okay?"

"What d'you mean—higher ground?"

"We don't stick around much, do we?" Jack got up and paced around. "We flash around, don't we? From place to place. In subtle timing, I mean."

MapHead watched Jack carefully. "Traveling's not so great. Families are better."

Jack snorted. "Yeah, right. That's why your dad's avoiding you."

"I mean it. There's a place you fit in. You're lucky."

"Yeah," Jack said, "lucky duck. I'm grounded except for boring old family outings; no one understands I need cash to, like, *travel* and stuff and go all the places I want to, plus I know about a million things and I can't do anything about them."

MapHead looked at him. "Wibble."

"There's one thing soon. It's my birthday."

"It is?"

"I wonder what'll foul it up," Jack said bitterly. "Probably it'll thunder."

It might, thought MapHead, do a great deal more than *that*. Feeling the wad of letters under the carpet with his foot, MapHead pictured Ada Leary's entrance in a rolling thundercloud raining stiff-looking envelopes.

Lightning flashed from her fingertips. The postman Crispin drove her vengeful chariot. Dogs of war snapped at her heels.

"What *was* that?" MapHead asked Jack, dreamily aware of a boom. "Is it thunder already?"

"Dunno," Jack said. "Sounds like something falling."

"JACK!" someone bawled up the stairwell. "JACK! I KNOW YOU'RE UP THERE!"

Lois put her head around the door. "Wonder what that noise was? Dining room, I think."

"JACK! I MEAN IT! GET HERE NOW!"

"You better get down there." Lois smiled sweetly. "I wouldn't be you, Jack Stamp."

At the bottom of the stairs they found the front door ajar and Martin Starkey waiting stupidly on the doorstep. The phone rang persistently in the hall. Martin Starkey smiled.

"I rang the bell. Is it a bad time?"

"What d'you want?" Jack glowered.

"I just came to tell you they're gone. I thought I better tell you."

"What are?"

"Those decks you wanted. Ben Pringle's brother sold 'em last night. Someone local. They paid cash and fetched 'em straight off."

"JACK! I WANT YOU! NOW!"

"But I told him I'd pay a deposit."

"He never said. They're gone now. I thought you'd like to know."

"Great. Brilliant. I love you." Jack closed the door emphatically on Martin Starkey's face. Smacking the phone off the hook on his way through the hall, Jack Stamp entered the dining room like anything might happen before he'd care.

"About time," Mrs. Stamp's voice said furiously. "What's the meaning of *this*?"

MapHead took up his position by the door jamb. He saw Mrs. Stamp put her hands on her hips. He heard the fury in her voice and knew it for what it was, almost—not quite— the last straw. The last straw but one for poor Jack.

"Meaning of what?" Jack asked.

"How can you ask? Look at this mess."

Things looked black for Jack. They looked pretty black mostly everywhere, now that MapHead came to look. A musty smell pervaded. There was black on the floor. Black in a fireplace MapHead had never even noticed before. A pile of black slabs on the carpet. Black over Valerie Stamp's armchairs. Black over Valerie Stamp.

"I never unblocked the chimney." Jack shrugged. "Why didn't you leave it alone?"

"I unblocked the fireplace to clean it," Valerie Stamp said wearily. "And what fell down inside? Apart from soot, I mean." She bent to pick up the black slabs—MapHead saw they were books—and threw them down one by one. "Geography, Mr. Rickman. Physics, Mr. Wiseman. Math, Mr. Rains. Chemistry, Miss Preston. Oh, and French and German. Mr. Brown, I think." Valerie Stamp looked up. "Just about every subject. Let's hope they're not current, eh, Jack? Else what would you be working in at school?"

"What—would I be working in?"

"Yes, Jack. How can you work with no books? Perhaps you'd like to show me your recent schoolwork. Then we'll know where we are. Although I *have* got some dates on these." She picked up a book between finger and thumb. "Here we are. Shales and Displacement. Monday, April 10th—what do you know? They're not so old, after all."

"Yes, they are. They're duff ones. It's all new coursework now."

"Sines, Cosines, and Tangents. Part One." Mrs. Stamp flipped a math book. "I wonder where Part Two is? Should we ask Mr. Rains?"

"It's like this," Jack affected a laugh. "It's stupid, really, what happened. Some of them's not that old. But what happened was, what happened was I—"

"Yes, Jack?" Valerie Stamp waited. "Why *is* your year eight schoolwork down the chimney? I'd really like to know."

Jack seemed to blank out suddenly. "Isn't that Pete Burns? Pete Burns, listening by the door?"

Mrs. Stamp whipped out to the doorway. MapHead blocked her vision, instantly, completely, with all the strength he had. It wasn't interfering. It wasn't going inside her mind. It was simply selecting what she saw. He had the right, after all. He didn't *have* to be seen.

Mrs. Stamp whipped back in. "This has nothing to do with Pete Burns. It has to do with *you*. But while we're on the subject." She strode rapidly out of vision. When she returned she had a book. MapHead strained at the door jamb. "While we're on the subject, take a look at *this*."

"*Pete Burns's Seafood Kitchen*." Jack considered the Lobster Bisque on the cover. "A cookery book? So?"

"So why's he called Pete Burns?"

"Our guest, you mean?"

"Who else?"

"Because it's his name? Pete. And Burns. It's not so unusual, is it?"

"Funny his name's the same name as this book in the cupboard."

"Hilarious. So what?"

"Jack. I think you know what I'm saying."

"No. I don't. Why don't you ask him yourself?"

"I don't really think I want to know. The thing is, how will it end?"

"*You* brought him home."

"I can't remember anything about it. Where does he come from? What should we do?"

Jack Stamp shrugged. "Like you care."

"Of *course* we care. You've changed, Jack. It's something to do with Pete Burns. Don't ask me how, but I know."

Jack Stamp shrugged again.

"What is the matter with you?"

"I'm a person. I want to be free."

Mrs. Stamp stared at her son. MapHead's heart raced. Everything seemed to be whirling, faster and faster, down a hole. Soon his whole life would go down it, and someone would put on the lid. And that would be—neatly—the end of it. Maybe not such a bad thing.

"That telephone number he gave me," Mrs. Stamp went on softly, "the one I asked him for so I could ring his parents? The international operator said there was no such number. Too many digits. They're all 490 numbers now. Even the first ones were wrong."

Jack Stamp edged his sooty books under a chair with his foot. His mother could ramble on ever so long, so long as the heat was off him. Happy to put the heat where it squarely belonged, on the shoulders of frail Pete Burns, Jack Stamp nodded in agreement.

"Yeah. I know. It's weird."

"He's very strange. Did you ever see him eat a plant?"

"A plant? No way." Jack made a face.

"That baby-sit you did. I didn't say, but Tanya rang. Why didn't you tell me Pete Burns ran a bath and flooded the room downstairs?"

"He had a bath. I don't know what else. I didn't know it ran over."

"Ran over is putting it mildly. Tanya said it looked as though he'd filled the bath right up and left the taps running. Water went straight through the floor. You didn't touch any makeup?"

"Makeup? Please. Why would I?"

"Tanya said it was everywhere, as though someone had *used every single thing* in her makeup bag upstairs."

"Crime of the century," Jack mugged, unpleasantly.

"And Maxie told her—it sounds mad, but

it was gone—Maxie told her he saw Pete Burns *eat her cyclamen.*"

"Her what?"

"Her cyclamen. A houseplant. Maxie saw him *eat* it."

"Oh. Gross. I mean, really?"

MapHead felt Lois coming downstairs before the scent of her reached him. He blocked her vision furiously as she blew past him like a dewberry-smelling wind, a wind he would follow if only—fat chance—she would let him.

"Mum. Quick. Take a look at this." Lois flung down a lunch box triumphantly. "Guess where I found it? No? *Under Pete Burns's bed.*"

Jack took a sharp breath. "Lois. Lois. Wait—"

"See?" Lois spilled the box out. "Thirty quid. My money I've been looking for?"

"What money?" Valerie Stamp asked. "Since when have you been looking for your money?"

"Ever since my money was missing? I *knew* I was right not to trust him."

"Lois, wait." Jack looked flushed. "Maybe it's not your money."

"Oh, right. Take *his* side." Lois appealed to her mother. "Can't you see what he's doing to Jack? What he's doing to all of us?"

"I don't know," Mrs. Stamp said helplessly.

"He loves Holly. He cheers me up. What *is* he doing to all of us?"

"Think about it," Lois said. "This weird kid arrives out of nowhere. Strange things go wrong in the house. *You* can't remember what you're doing. Jack goes crazy, and no one asks why? And now he takes my money? My money I earned at Mandeville's?"

"What do you mean at Mandeville's? Since when do you work at a nightclub?"

Lois stuck her chin out. "I'm waitressing. I told you."

"Just a minute. You most certainly did not. You can get on that phone right away and tell them you won't be in. It's a good thing your father's gone out. Don't think your father's going to—" Valerie Stamp stopped suddenly.

In listening, gobsmacked, to the whirling black hole of suspicion and countersuspicion that threatened to suck them all in, MapHead had drifted out in full view of the open doorway. In the heat of the moment they saw him. Naked but for his clothes, full but for utter emptiness, MapHead stood in the doorway and stared at his adoptive family. His adoptive family stared back. MapHead spread his arms in a kind of mute appeal.

"Show them, then," Jack ordered. "Go on, then. *Map it up*."

They could have asked him anything. Anything at all. Obediently, MapHead set up a flow of maps over his scalp and face that would have defeated an artist to capture. He centered mainly on Spain. It seemed like the heartland he yearned for. Then he ran Antarctica: Mount Erebus; the Mertz Glacier; Cape Crozier, where the emperor penguins huddled that time when he'd longed to join in, but hadn't been able to, really. One of a kind when the icecap froze, he would never really fit in. The plots and contours rose and fell, swifter than MapHead thought them. The Amery Ice Shelf; Mount Terror; the Beardmore Glacier; Shackleton Inlet; Elephant Island; the Weddell Sea. The coldest names on earth.

MapHead stood in the doorway of the house called Rising Sun, on Gough Street, Rubytown, and glowed like an Antarctic sunset. The family called Stamp stood and watched him. And watched and watched and watched.

THE MULTI AGAIN

"Here. I brought you some breakfast."

Jack Stamp took off his Walkman. He waited a moment, then deposited his offering of cold Marmite toast in sandwich wrap and a carton of orange juice on the oily concrete deck next to MapHead. MapHead didn't turn around.

"I *told* 'em you didn't take Lois's money. I told 'em it was mine. Wish I hadn't, now. Now they think I took it. It *is* Lois's money, but what am I going to tell them?"

Jack Stamp paused. He looked at Map-Head. MapHead continued staring out over the eight o'clock town. The past two nights he'd snuck home to curl up beside Holly's cot when the family Stamp was asleep, but he didn't want Jack to know that. Daytime, he'd

The Multi Again

spent up the multi. That was the way it had gone. But it couldn't go on that way much longer. Well and truly outcast now, he might as well make his move.

"The thing is, I only borrowed it."

Jack Stamp squatted beside MapHead. Cars spiraled up to Level C behind them. The town below was waking up. A large delivery lorry nosed its way down Fore Street. The air was crisp, the sky light, beyond the stink of exhaust. It was going to be a nice day. Another nice day without MapHead.

"All right, I shouldn't have done it," Jack Stamp admitted. "I don't know why I've been doing weird things. It's just, I want something to *happen*." He looked at MapHead. "I've started a rap. Want to hear it?"

MapHead stared out over the town. A small vein pulsed behind his ear. The worst thing was feeling lonely. Sticking-out kind of lonely, like a sore thumb or an ugly piece of furniture someone put out for the trash collectors. Map-Head sighed. One of the family. As if. A map-flashing, plant-eating, mind-bending *traveler* like him. Please. What did he expect?

"Mum reported you missing last night," Jack said. "They wanted a photo. And a name that wasn't Pete Burns? The policeman asked me who I thought you really were."

Jack Stamp glanced across at MapHead. Then he unwrapped the Marmite toast and slowly began to eat it himself. "Like, what am I going to tell them? You're a super-powerful, inter-dimensional traveler, sleeping rough up at the multi?"

Jack polished off the Marmite toast. He lanced the carton of orange juice with its straw and began to drink it. "Anyway," he said, "it might be good if you rang 'em. Mum and Dad, I mean. Tell 'em you've gone to Greece. Least then they might stop worrying."

MapHead inclined his head. He might have been nodding agreement.

Jack Stamp rose, slapping crumbs off his Hubert Sewell blazer. "Got to keep 'em happy. You have to, really, don't you? That's why I'm going to school. I'm just, like, marking time?"

MapHead gave no answer, nor any indication that he was listening. The rumble and growl of parking cars filled the hollow-sounding car-decks. Doors slammed. Office workers filed busily out toward the stained concrete stairwell. Others waited impatiently for the lift. Jack Stamp took it all in. Plenty of people around. But none of them looking at *him*.

"Here," he said, "cop this." Striking a pose he began to intone:

The Multi Again

"Now we're *out*
and all *alone*
Say Maps
where *do*
you keep
your *home*

Is it Cool Street,
is it *rude*
is it somewhere
in the *'hood*—

'Hood, that's *neighborhood*, see?" Jack went
on, intoning rapidly, popping his knees with
the rhythm:

"Is it smokin'
is it *funky*
up—up—up the
up the *multi* . . .

Multi-*plicity*
in the
inner city
multi-*tud*inous
mighty-*rude*-of-us
multi-*mill*ionaire
what me
I should care—"

He stopped uncertainly. "Then the refrain comes in.

> On cuh-cuh Cool Street
> *Say Maps!*
> On cuh-cuh Cool Street
> *Say Maps!*
>
> multi-farious
> multi-*scarious*
> multi-lateral
> multi-*splateral*
> multi-*cellular*
> dig how *well* ya are
> On cuh-cuh Cool Street—
> *Say Maps!*

Then I name-check DJ BlackJack. I'm working on the rest." Jack Stamp looked at MapHead. "So tell me so far. What do you think?"

MapHead shifted very slightly. Stiff legged and straight backed, he might have sat that way for hours. Jack took the slight shift kindly.

"Cool, isn't it? Not finished yet. But cool." Jack sighed. "It's a sickener Ben Pringle's brother sold those decks. I could've mixed a backing." He checked his watch, then shouldered his school bag reluctantly. "I'm going to school now, worse luck. I'll bring you some dinner tonight." He walked around the front of MapHead to make sure he understood. "Dinner tonight, okay? I'll be round about eight, maybe half past?"

MapHead stirred. "Don't bother."

"It's no bother." Jack sighed again. "Crappy detention every day this week to catch up with classwork I missed. Plus I get no credits. Plus I have to pay for new schoolbooks."

MapHead looked out over Rubytown. "Anyway. Soon it's your birthday."

"I'm not having any birthday. I have to see Ada Leary instead. That's what Dad said, anyway."

"Grim." MapHead thawed very slightly.

"It's more than grim, it's tragic." Jack Stamp backed away. "I have to go now. See you later, okay?"

"I'll be round tonight to guard Holly," MapHead said rustily. "Don't bother bringing me food."

"Why are you always guarding Holly? Holly's all right. What can happen?" Jack Stamp shrugged. "Whatever you like. I'll see you. I'll have some food in my room."

MapHead considered the waking town while Jack Stamp walked away. It was a town it hurt him to look at. His mother and half brother lived here. Somewhere, out over the houses, were the bedrooms where they'd slept. A kitchen they'd just had breakfast in. A front door they'd just walked out of. Their lives were complete without him. He wouldn't—would *not*—interfere. This had to be the last time. The last time he'd come to Rubytown, MapHead decided, as Jack Stamp's footsteps died.

Suddenly Jack was back. Jack's face was in MapHead's face, his anxious eyes on Map-Head's. "Soon we're off on our travels, aren't we? Flashing from place to place. No limits, right? You and me. *Just you and me together.*"

Jack's fevered face searched MapHead's. His words had come out in a jumble no one else could have understood.

"We're only, like, treading water just now. Aren't we? We're travelers, right? We don't stay long, wherever we go. And we jump—*flash*—and we're somewhere else, maybe Mauritius or Africa?"

MapHead looked at Jack. "Go to school," he said, evenly. "We're only treading water."

"Hello? Is that Mrs. Stamp?"

"Speaking."

"It's me, Pete Burns. I'm phoning from

Greece. I'm with Mum and Dad. So don't worry."

A longish silence. "How did you get there? Who are you, really?"

"Really I do hypnosis. I've been on Hypnosis Holidays. They place you with other people's parents? Now I'm at home I'm fine. My mum and dad say thanks."

"I don't understand. What do you mean— Hypnosis Holidays?"

"So if you think you saw funny stuff, remember it's only a trick. Things'll settle down now I'm gone. And your family's the best. 'Specially Holly. And I want to say thank you very much."

"Hello? Are your parents there? I don't remember volunteering for any holiday scheme." Valerie Stamp shook the phone. "Hello? Pete Burns? Are you there?"

After finally replacing the phone, Mrs. Stamp sat down. How extraordinary she shouldn't remember a holiday scheme she took part in. How extraordinary she thought she saw squiggles and lines all over that boy's face. It must have been the hypnosis. *That* would explain a few things. How extraordinary he should suddenly ring her from Greece. *Things should settle down now I'm gone.* Mrs. Stamp made herself a large pot of Earl Grey tea and sat down with it. Then she opened the cupboard again and took out *Pete Burns's Seafood Kitchen*.

Pete Burns. Or whoever he was. What an extraordinary interlude. She started to smile at a number of things. The puppies Pete Burns had said he'd saved when he lost his hair; the way Pete Burns was—supposedly—too intelligent to go to school; the way he'd caused that rumpus at the pool, seemingly without meaning to; the way he nursed Holly so carefully and mended her dolphin mobile when it broke; the way he took everything so literally, you had to be careful what you said. It really was too silly. Valerie Stamp wiped her cheek. Was she laughing or crying? Certainly Pete Burns had been very strange indeed. The funny thing was, she missed him.

On impulse she called her son in. "Jack! Fancy the Mixed Seafood Risotto tonight?" She showed him the colorful picture on page ten of the *Seafood Kitchen*. "That was Pete Burns. Ringing from Greece. He's met his parents and they're fine."

"Greece. That's great." Jack Stamp eyed his mother. "Seafood Risotto looks good."

"So." Valerie Stamp straightened and brushed back her hair. "I don't know how he got there. I'm not even really sure what's happened. But it seems there's no need to worry, after all."

"You worry too much, Mum," Jack told her. "Sit down and finish your tea." He took the cookery book off her. "I'll make Seafood Risotto. It looks pretty easy, don't you think?"

Mrs. Stamp let Jack steer her into her chair. She hugged him before he got away. "Did you know you were heavier than Holly when you were born?"

"How heavy was Holly?" Jack asked.

"Seven pounds, twelve ounces."

"And how heavy was I?"

"Eight pounds, ten ounces."

"Was Dad glad when you had me?"

"Your dad? He was over the moon." Jack seemed to tower over her somehow. She was comforting him. He knew it. She couldn't quite get through to him. Something was stopping her—what?

"I'm going to be nicer to Holly in the future." Jack smiled. He was making a gesture. Saying, I know what you're doing, and thanks. "I'll come back when it's time to start cooking, okay?"

"Okay." Mrs. Stamp smiled. But something about Jack chilled her. His knowingness made him cold. At least he was going to school.

Things'll settle down now I'm gone. Perhaps, with time, they would.

Valerie Stamp finished her tea. Then she got up and took a pack of Atlantic prawns out of the freezer. She brought out some rice and washed it. Then she dialed Rubytown Constabulary.

"Hello? Police? Yes. It's about a missing person. The young man calling himself Pete Burns? We registered him the other night. The thing is, I've just heard from him, and—Mrs. V. A. Stamp. Gough Street. Yes. No. Pete Burns. It seems he's with his parents. That's right. *He isn't missing anymore. . . .*"

16

STEALING TIME

MapHead smelled the air. The late night stroll to the Stamps' house had had a special quality about it. The air was still and sweet. Everything seemed to listen and lean—the cemetery yews excepted—to MapHead as he passed. The pelican crossing winked feebly; the traffic lights ordered stop and go, down the long road empty of cars; the old soldiers guarding the cemetery walls popped up on cue, their ghostly faces spoiling as no one inspected their parade. MapHead wasn't about to. He had better fish to fry. All the same, it wouldn't do to get there too early. Not before he could be certain the Stamps had retired to bed. MapHead made it a rule.

The Nuns' Pond had looked sweetly cool under the moonlight. Frogs chirruped somewhere

around it, probably glad he—MapHead—
would never again sit on their tadpoles. The
air had a quality of good-bye in it that made
every second thing precious, like something
you saw for the first—or last—time in your
life. Turning the corner on Gough Street,
MapHead wondered how much longer he
would stay. Long enough to be certain Jack
would watch over Holly. Long enough, at
least, to give Jack his memories back.

MapHead registered the dirty white van
outside Jack's house without much surprise.
What *did* surprise him was the flickering flash-
light inside the house. And the open front
door.

Immediately after MapHead entered the
hall a large young man surprised him with the
family Stamp's TV. MapHead stepped swiftly
aside. In not allowing the large young man to
see him, he would have time to work out what
was happening. The large young man passed
him closely with the telly. MapHead watched
him take it down the steps and load it into the
van. The steady drip of surprise was suddenly
overtaken by a stronger feeling of suspicion.
Something was occurring, MapHead felt sure.
Not for nothing had he watched *Inspector
Morse* and *The Bill*.

As soon as the large young man hopped up

the steps and reentered the Stamps' living room, MapHead whisked the telly out of the van and carried it back to the house. He met the young man head-on in the hall with the family Stamp's VCR.

"I can understand why you're doing this," MapHead told the burglar. "You must have had a rotten life to have to do this. People don't understand you prob'ly don't have a job or any money. The thing is, they're not rich or anything. They've only got one TV."

The burglar looked at the telly. Floating in midair around waist height, it seemed to be telling him it understood why he'd pinched it.

"Are you Rob?" MapHead went on severely. "Big Shout 2's big brother?"

It even knew his name!!! The VCR tilted in Rob's nerveless fingers. Something caught it as it fell. A deeply confusing moment passed. Then Big Shout 2's big brother, Rob, ran for his van like a man desperate for the toilet. He didn't know what it was that had happened, but whatever it was, he didn't like it. Something made him turn before he jumped into the van, something—a silhouette—up on the roof. It brought him up short with his heart in his mouth, what wasn't in it already. Someone standing up there like that. On the very edge of the roof. A person could get himself *killed*.

"Don't do it!" Thoroughly spooked by the sound of his own voice, Rob Smith heard himself shouting. "Straight up, it isn't worth it! Do yourself a favor and get back inside again, matey!"

Expecting something else to go wrong every second minute, Rob Smith jumped into the dirty white van he'd "borrowed" from Rippons Family Butcher and roared away. Maybe he'd pack it in for a while. This kind of stuff was too weird. If tellies could finger him now, *what could a stolen van do?*

MapHead watched him go. He coolly removed the key from the door that Rob Smith had gotten in with, and hung it back on its hook; Jack's key he lost some time ago. He set down the VCR in the hall next to the rescued telly. Then he went out on the step and looked up. What had Rob the robber been shouting about? Matey? Where? Up on the roof. There *was* someone up there—wasn't there?

"Jack! Is that you? I said, *Jack!*"

It was—it looked like—Jack Stamp. Jack Bradley Stamp on the edge—the *very* edge— of the roof. With only the whole of the known world and a very hard pavement beneath him.

"Jack! Wait! Don't move!"

MapHead tore up the steps into the hall; up the stairs to the landing; through the door into

Jack's room. The swivel-round Velux window onto the roof had been swiveled around, all right. Jack had gotten out onto the roof, all right. And stood there, all right, so far.

"So." MapHead swung out onto the roof.

"Rob Smith was taking our telly," Jack said, matter-of-factly. "But it doesn't matter to us."

"It doesn't?"

"No, because we're going any minute. You took long enough. I've been waiting here for ages."

"Stand back a bit, I should," MapHead advised Jack worriedly. How strong was the gutter? Jack was standing, MapHead saw, in the very place he'd stood himself, not so very long ago—when he'd launched off to visit the penguins, that time before he'd been outcast, when *joining in* had still been an option. "Jack. Stand back, why don't you?"

"Why?"

"You might as well sit down, if you want." He could see now, Jack's face had a fixed look. "We're not quite ready yet."

"Yes, we are," Jack said. "I've been ready a long time, me. I want to go where you go. Like when you saw the penguins? And now you're here at last."

"I'm here if you want me, but *please*, Jack Stamp, sit down." MapHead edged carefully toward him. Jack looked distinctly shaky. How long had he stood in the gutter with a wandering, half-puzzled look on his face, and the whole dark world before him, and nothing at all except an idea of waiting for MapHead holding him back? Poised to leap off the roof, Jack Stamp had the look of a bungee jumper. Only thing was, no bungee.

"It's you and me," Jack said simply. *"Just you and me together, okay?"*

"No! Jack Stamp! You can't!"

"It's too late to stop me now." Jack Stamp swayed out, swayed back. "I'm going places you go." He smiled. "In *traveling* time, all right?"

MapHead gained the chimney, swung down and around beside it, and reaching Jack, clipped his legs around Jack's. Jack smiled down serenely, as though MapHead's move were the last in a complicated game plan designed to bring them together at the very point they'd arrived at.

"Ready?"

"No! Jack! *Don't!*"

Still smiling, Jack jumped off the roof. His legs tangled in Jack's legs, MapHead fell off the roof with him. Nothing much else disturbed the small hours. Outside a butcher's shop two miles away, Rob Smith reversed a dirty white van back into its parking space, then legged it into the night. The front door of the Stamp house stood open onto the street. A cat wandered in, and then out again. The television sat blankly in the hall where MapHead had left it. The dog Weg slept dreamlessly in the kitchen. Mr. and Mrs. Stamp snored upstairs. Holly turned, too hot, in her crib, her blankets up over her head.

The moon shone; the garden settled; the green-winking night ticked and glowed. Nothing much more disturbed it after the complicated knot of arms and legs and bodies dropped silently off the edge of the roof and disappeared in a flash of light that died on the promise of morning.

17

A FAMILY AFFAIR

"Wow!" Jack called, in free fall. "We're going somewhere amazing, right?"

"We're not going anywhere at all." MapHead looked severe.

Jack Stamp saw a darkened bedroom from a point somewhere over the bed. "I'm floating. How am I floating?"

This is subtle time, MapHead seemed to tell him. *We can do anything we like.*

"But why can't we visit jungles an' stuff? I want to go places you've been, places with mountains and ghosts — "

"Jack Bradley Stamp." MapHead looked angry. He'd never, Jack realized, really seen MapHead angry. "I'm going to show you something."

The boy in the bed beneath them stirred.

212

Somehow they seemed to dip closer. The boy in the bed was fair with a radical haircut. His face was marked by the deepest sleep, the deepest passing dreams. Posters looked down over his bed head. A pair of jeans stood on the floor like he'd just jumped out of them. He could have been almost any age. It was hard to tell in the dark.

"I'm strange. I'll always be strange." Map-Head whispered a subtle song straight into Jack Stamp's heart. *"This is my half brother, Kenny. I can't know him. You've got two sisters. Be glad."*

"But why can't you know him?" Jack asked.

"He'd change, the way you changed," the answer rang back, like an echo. *"I can't ever really know him. Because of what happened to you."*

Jack Stamp looked down on Kenny and wondered, What must it be like? A brother you can't ever know? He pictured Lois and Holly. They were pretty annoying sometimes. But they really weren't that bad.

The bedroom scene shifted and changed. This time the bed was a double, empty but for a fair-headed woman with silky-looking arms thrown wide over a rose-covered duvet. Jack dipped down. He smelled her. She smelled like—

"This is my mother, Kay," the whisper ran on. *"I can know her only in dreams. You've got your mother. Be glad."*

Jack Stamp looked at Kay. Fairer by a mile than his own mother, she looked kindly, like her. And pretty.

Again the bedroom scene shifted. A large lady in a hair net lay gently snoring in bed. Again MapHead whispered his song:

"I'm strange, I'll always be strange. This is my grandmother, Frida. I can't know her. You've got your dad. Be glad."

"But you've got your dad," Jack seemed to say.

"We've got each other." MapHead smiled.

The bedroom shrank and grew darker. Bold things rushed by in dreams. A light, Jack thought, came and went. Again they looked down on a bedroom. A bedroom much smaller, this time. No bookshelves decorated these walls. No friendly posters looked down.

"No love no home this summer," ran the whisper. *"This is Big Shout 2. His foster home can't love him. His mother doesn't want him. He stays off school and spray paints walls. He doesn't know what to do. He hasn't had a fair start. Not,"* ran the whisper, *"like you."*

Jack Stamp looked down on Big Shout 2. His mind enclosed the lies he'd told, the lies

Big Shout 2 had told, too. He'd pushed him around. He shouldn't have. The things he knew had made him mad for money—for everything—somehow. It didn't matter anymore. What mattered most was family.

"It's not his fault." It really wasn't. Map-Head spread his arms. *"He doesn't fit in. Like me."*

Jack Stamp felt himself nodding. "Can we go now?" he asked.

The poor bedroom shrank away. Big skies rushed down to receive them. This time the light flashed them high on a hill under the moon. The flower fields skirting Rubytown lay like a bedspread beneath them. Away toward the distant north and west a brave line of wind turbines sticklebacked a ridge.

Jack could see his own house. "Wait! I don't want to go home yet!"

"Home," thrilled poor MapHead, "*home.*"

Home. Jack sensed how much the word meant. "I'm glad I saw your family," he said. "Your mother looks really nice."

"My mother's human, my father isn't." MapHead almost broke down. "Now you know why I'll *never* fit in."

"You're special, not strange." Jack sat down next to him, touching him. "MapHead. You should be glad."

"I should be glad. I *am* glad. It's just, I have to get used to it. I'm going to be lonely a long time."

"Why would you be lonely," Jack said, "when you can always come and see me?"

MapHead smiled in a watery way. Then he smelled the air. "Thunder's coming. Feel it?"

"Purple," Jack said, "it feels—purple, somehow. I don't like it. Let's—"

"LET'S NOT!"

"What's that voice? Where's it come from?" Jack looked around him fearfully. A green hill. A thunderstorm. Something about to happen.

"MAPHEAD! STAY WHERE YOU ARE!"

"What is it?" Jack whimpered. "Is it God?"

"No." MapHead straightened. "My father."

MAPHEAD'S TRIAL

"*Thou art so powerful . . .*" MapHead searched the sky, remembering the lines from *The Snow Queen* he read once, so long ago. "*Thou art so powerful that I know thou canst twist all the winds of the world into a thread . . .*"

The night sky heaved and flashed. The brightest of lights alighted.

"*. . . and if the pilot loosens one knot of it he will have a favorable wind.*" Powers stood before them in all his awesome glory.

"Dad."

"MapHead."

"This is Jack."

"Jack Bradley Stamp, I know. Excuse us, Jack? While we talk?" Powers placed a hand over Jack Stamp's face and Jack Stamp closed his eyes. Powers's suit flashed silver under the moon as he turned to MapHead.

"Dad"—MapHead raised a hand—"I know what you're going to say."

"MapHead. I don't think you do."

"You're going to ask me what I've done to Jack Stamp's mind."

"*What have you done to Jack Stamp's mind?*" Powers seemed to grow. His voice took on a dangerous note, his eyes a dangerous glow. "*Now is the time to account for anything and everything you've done, in this world or any other.*"

"Okay, Dad, the thing is I—"

"*You interfered. I warned you. You had no right.*"

"I've learned, Dad. I know. I understand what I am." MapHead swelled, himself. "And I'm making it right without you."

"*You force me to intervene before seven years is up. Before seven weeks is up, you ask me what you should do. Is this the way you manage on your own?*"

"I know it doesn't look good, Dad. But I know what I'm doing now."

"*In every corner of every world you pursue me, calling for help.*" Powers's teeth flashed. His body crackled with energy. "*MapHead. I must ask you. Is Jack Stamp's mind his own?*"

"Not quite yet. But it will be."

"And have you understood?"

"Understood what?"

"What else? The nature of power."

MapHead stared levelly at his father. It seemed a battle of giants. "The nature of power," he said evenly, "is such that it cannot be understood."

Thunder grumbled somewhere. Powers seemed to shrink. "Well and good." He smiled. "My dear and only son."

"It's lonely, isn't it?" said MapHead, after a moment. "Being us, I mean."

Powers nodded slowly. "Very lonely," he said.

Exchanging thoughts only they could understand they sat awhile enjoying each other, like arctic terns that range thousands of miles and only touch earth now and then.

"Was it you, Dad?" MapHead asked.

"Me, what?" murmured Powers.

"The man in purple. In Sparta."

"Sparta?"

"'It is better to travel than to arrive.' Come off it, Dad. The sage."

"Purple for wisdom. Choose your own way." Powers encircled his son with an arm. "You don't need me to tell you."

"Not now, I don't," said MapHead, flushing

his scalp with happy maps of Rubytown.

Powers traced the outlines with his finger. *Well-Met Cross. Gladsome Lane. Heartslove Place. Rejoice-and-Be-Glad. Welcome Break. The Happy Shopper, Glee Street.*

"Did you see your mother?" he asked.

"I saw her. I didn't interfere."

Powers was thoughtful. "Maybe I'll look in myself."

After Powers finally flashed away on the wind with the time fixed for six years, nine months, one week, seven hours, and forty minutes precisely until they met again, MapHead remembered Jack Stamp. Still mesmerized by Powers, Jack Stamp smiled mildly in subtle time. Subtle time that, suddenly, seemed to have an edge. *Hurry,* ran the vibe. *Hurry, for heaven's sake.*

MapHead took Jack's face in his hands and sucked away all those things he'd lent him — the pictures he'd smoothed in with Jack's pictures; the cave; the desert; the reading-day picnic; the big-sky country he'd grown up with. The memories flashed back faster as he remembered them, replaced by Jack Stamp's own. My memories. My lifetime. My knowledge. MapHead pulled them back. *Remember it back to me.*

Jack Stamp opened his eyes. "Don't take it all away, will you?"

MapHead jumped, surprised. "I have to make you forget."

"No," Jack said, "I can handle it."

"Everything?"

"Some of it, anyway. *Please* don't make me forget. I want to remember —"

"Want to remember what?"

"You," Jack said, "I want to remember *you*."

MapHead covered Jack's face with his hand in a gesture he rarely employed. When he pulled away his hand, Jack was smiling. Some things Jack would *never* forget. MapHead smiled in the knowledge, too.

"It's good that's done, 'cos we have to hurry." MapHead smelled the vibe. "Can't you feel the pull?"

"What pull?"

The light built all around them. *Hurry. For heaven's sake.*

"There's something wrong. *That* pull."

"What d'you mean, something's wrong?" Jack felt the pull as it took him. Already he felt himself *traveling* as the light built quickly and engulfed them. "What is it?" Jack heard himself screaming as MapHead tumbled away into space toward a destination all his own. "MapHead, what is it, what's happening? *I don't understand! What's wrong?*"

Holly, drummed Jack's mind through space

for the merest split second of subtle time in the flash from place to place. *Holly. Hurry. For Holly's sake. Hurry. For hurry's sake. Holly.*

19

WAKING . . . SHAKING

"I don't understand!" Jack found himself shouting in Holly's room. "I don't understand! What's wrong?"

Where, for a start, was the baby? He felt around in Holly's crib, panic coursing through him as he did it. He tore off Holly's bedclothes. There she was, squashed, at the bottom. Very hot. Bright red in the face. *And not breathing.*

Jack scooped her up and shook her. What to do next? *Hurry, for Holly's sake, hurry.* He laid her on the floor. Covered her mouth and nose with his mouth. Breathed in quick, little breaths. Applied two fingers to her chest. Pumped them quickly up and down. Not too much pressure for a baby. Breathed little breaths. Pumped two fingers. Breathed little breaths. Pumped two fingers. Again and again and again.

223

He didn't know how long he did it. Suddenly Holly stiffened, spluttered—and wailed, a great choking wail that died, came back, then quickly climbed to a full-on scream of annoyance. Feeling slightly sick, Jack held Holly to him, enjoying her struggling body, her irritable legs, her sticky-feeling chin, and everything else about her. Close call, or what? A big hand for *Dr. Gillian's Encyclopedia of Childcare*. Some shreds of it had jumped across. Good thing MapHead read so much. How else had he known what to do?

Jack was still shaking when, holding Holly closely, he cradled her bravely next door. His parents' room stood open. The clock told a quarter to seven.

"Mum. Dad. Here's Holly." He laid her on the bed.

His parents were stirring already. Valerie Stamp hit the clock. "Jack. Is she wet or something?"

"Probably." Jack kissed her and smiled. "Who cares?"

"You look flushed. Are you all right?"

Jack Stamp looked down on his early-morning mother. A million thoughts rushed by him. He could have said, "No, I'm not. Holly almost died." It had been a pretty strange night. He'd dreamed—had he?—he

224

jumped off the roof. It had seemed pretty real, but it couldn't be. Else he wouldn't be standing here in his parents' bedroom.

He rubbed his head. Then he said, "I sleep-walked into Holly's room. I dreamed she couldn't breathe." A little knowledge was a good thing. Way less threatening, this way. "She's too hot, Mum. You should get rid of that duvet. Put her to bed so that her feet touch the bottom of the crib? That way she can't wriggle down and get overheated."

Valerie Stamp sat up. "You're absolutely right. That's what they said on that program. That program the other night? I was thinking about it, anyway. I should've done it before." She scooped Holly up in her arms and fed her, warmly, in the folds of her nightdress. She reached across and squeezed Jack's arm. "Thank you, Jack," she said.

Jack Stamp relaxed at last. He had the feeling—certain, somehow—that Holly would be fine. It wouldn't happen again, because his mother would take steps to stop it. Through him, she would know. Through MapHead, *he* knew. The danger had been averted. Map-Head, in his own—a *MapHeadish* way—had guarded Holly well.

"Jack." Jack's father stirred and sat up. "Time to push the boat out. Happy birthday, old son."

"I'm not having any birthday," Jack said mechanically. "I've got to see Ada Leary instead."

"Ada Leary!" Jack's father lay back and changed color. "Of course! He's got to see Ada Leary!" Strange hiccups shook the bed. "Ada . . . Leary . . . instead!"

"For heaven's sake, get on with it." Valerie Stamp kissed Jack. "Happy birthday, love."

"He's got to see . . . Ada Leary!" Jack's dad roared. *"Good luck! It's Saturday, you twonk!"*

"Oh," Jack said. "Then what—"

"Lift that sheet up. That sheet over there." Alan Stamp gestured weakly in the general direction of a large, sheet-covered lump in the corner. "Yes. That sheet. Go on."

Jack went over and lifted it. When he saw what was under it he felt kind of sick and *overblown,* somehow. It was too much. He'd been such a pain. Hadn't it been sold, already? How much had it cost, anyhow?

"Dad," he said, "you shouldn't have."

"I know, but I did it anyway."

"It was you." Jack stared. "When Starkers came to tell me they'd gone. Ben Pringle's brother only sold 'em to *you.*"

"I knocked him down a bit." Jack's dad grinned. "You'll have to earn it, mind."

Jack Stamp swallowed hugely. When he saw the whole kit—the twin decks plus mixer—his dad *had gone out of his way* to make sure that he—Jack—had on his birthday, his chest filled with the knowledge that his father loved and understood him—*had* loved him, of course—all along. There would always be Lois and Holly. But love and attention weren't divided like a cake at a picnic. However much got eaten up, there would *always* be enough to go around.

"Dad, you're *brilliant*. I can't believe you did this. Not after—"

"All the aggro you caused? Not half so much as I did, when I was your age."

"You did? I mean—make some hassles?"

"No excuses. But I was no angel. And you're worth three of me."

"I am?"

Jack's dad nodded slowly. "Underneath. I know."

After they'd hugged each other quite a while Jack held out his hand. "Hey, Dad," he said, "gimme five."

Alan Stamp grinned. He slapped his son's hand with his. "I'll give you ten if you'll get that thing out of here by tonight. We've lived with it in the bedroom so long, I practically kiss it good night."

"It's cool, Dad. Really the best." Jack Stamp struck a pose behind his twin turntables: "This is DJ BlackJack, Prince of the Mix, givin' out hardcore, techno, dance-zone, rap. Check it out. With the most—the coolest—sounds around, can you afford not to?" Jack popped his knees and grinned. "I'll make it pay its way, Dad. I'll do parties when I'm good. Rappin' Jack Stamp. Who could resist?"

"I could, for starters."

"I'm sorry. I know I've been out of order. I think I've been a bit mad."

"Loud music'll do it to you. Want me to jam the volume on that thing?"

"I mean it, I'm really sorry." Jack came over and sat down. "I did some bad things, I don't know why." The signs of strain stood in his face. Good and bad had fought in Jack Stamp. But the outcome had not been in doubt. "Nothing so bad I can't put it right, though. I think Pete Burns thought I took things. One time when I went up the multi? I *wish* I'd found that door key."

"You could have dropped it anywhere. No sense in worrying about it now." Alan Stamp climbed out of bed and clumped his way downstairs. "I'll put the kettle on. No," he called back, "it's no trouble. I didn't want breakfast in bed."

"Aw, Dad . . ."

"Only joking!" Dad called.

Dozy with milk, Holly looked up. Valerie Stamp set her down. "It's like you've been away." She looked at Jack, then hugged him. "I can't tell how, but you're back."

"I really am," Jack said, both eyes shut really tight. "I wanted to, like, do stuff. Stuff like travel around? But everything I want's right here."

"You'll want to get away someday."

"Someday's plenty of time."

"Jimmy-Jack Stamp, you're a strange one." His mother hugged him some more.

"Enough, already." Jack looked mock-severe. *Mappers*, he thought, *can you see this?* "How can I keep my cred with everyone *hugging* me all the time?"

Released from the kitchen, the dog Weg bounded upstairs and greeted them sloppily. Lois's bedroom door banged. A howl resounded downstairs. Alan Stamp's voice rose on an anguished note:

"WHAT'S THIS FRONT DOOR DOING OPEN? WHAT GENIUS LEFT THE VIDEO RECORDER IN THE HALL? WE'RE DAMN LUCKY NO ONE'S PINCHED IT!"

"STOP SHOUTING!" Lois shouted crossly, coming around the door with a present for

Jack in one hand and a toothbrush in the other. "EVERYBODY'S ALWAYS SHOUT-ING IN THIS HOUSE!"

"I wish I knew what was going on. I SAID, I WISH I KNEW WHAT WAS GOING ON. DID YOU KNOW THIS MISSING KEY'S ON ITS HOOK? ANYONE KNOW HOW IT GOT THERE?"

"I love this family, you know?" Jack threw back his head and allowed himself to laugh. "I wouldn't want any other."

"Business as usual, then." Valerie Stamp smiled. "Happy birthday, Jack."

20

HOUSE OF TOMORROW

Power is lonely. Power stands apart.

MapHead worked it out slowly. Round and round, in circles. The reason he wouldn't fit in.

Power stands apart. I have power. Therefore, I'm lonely.

The wind blew keenly over the Sierra Nevada. The plants on the patio of the house called Casa Mañana knocked softly together as it reached them. Sheltered by the wall around a small pool, bright with inflatables, the girl on the patio pulled on a colored robe and turned the page of her book. The holiday hacienda had been neatly tucked into a fold in the hills. The scrubland reminded MapHead of his one-time home in Arizona. In fact, it was southern Spain. Somewhere near Granada. MapHead had crossed a mountain or three before he'd found the house.

He watched from the hillside opposite as a tanned boy crossed the patio with a tray of tall pink drinks. He set the tray down on a table. The girl sat up and took off her sunglasses and laughed at something the boy said. The pool threw lights on her dark blonde hair. "Perry," she called, "I'm warning you." She threw a cushion at Perry. He threw the cushion back, not in anger at all. The girl pushed him. She laughed a lot. They knew each other well.

A middle-aged woman joined them and laughed a lot at them both. Perry picked up the tray and held it out. "Here, Mom—have a drink."

Casa Mañana. It meant House of Tomorrow. MapHead shifted on his rock. He watched the girl on the patio thoughtfully. Close enough to hear what she said, far enough to feel the separation in time and space, he wasn't about to break Future rules or any others. Here, at least, there were clear boundaries, and he—MapHead—meant to stay inside them. He would enjoy the scene while he could. No hint of his presence must escape. The House of Tomorrow must never feel his footstep on its threshold, a footstep that, as yet, couldn't—hadn't—ever been there. Map-Head sighed. Future rules were complex.

Along with love, responsibility, knowledge, friendship, and just about anything *else* you cared to think of.

"Holly—don't—get off! Careful, you'll spill your drink!" Perry straightened, panting, a cushion ready in his hand, should Holly hit him with hers.

"No chance." Future Holly plumped down on a sun-bed, laughing. "Too good to waste on you." She eyed the surrounding hills over the top of her long pink drink. As the level dropped, she quietened. "It's funny, I—"

"What?"

"Oh, nothing. I just thought of something, that's all."

Future Holly would be sixteen or seventeen at this stage, MapHead decided, from his hillside perch looking down on her. If only Jack Stamp could see his sister. Enough, for the moment, that *he* could. Enough that she was safe and well—and would be throughout her childhood, now that he could *see*, beyond doubt, she'd come through it.

"What sort of something?" Perry wanted to know.

"Oh, just this thing when I was small," Future Holly said, reflectively. "These stickers I had in my room? I spent ages and ages staring at them every night before I went to sleep, and I can still remember *every single sticker,* you know? And the light always seemed to be pink. I had a pig eating a chocolate eclair, Father Christmas, a toothy snake, a one-eyed monster—an alien, I think—in a spaceship, just about everything you could think of, on my white chest of drawers, and I used to, you know, think they were *magic* or something. And once my brother told me—"

"Your brother told you what?"

"Oh, it's just my brother. Once he told me that they *were.* Magic, I mean. 'Specially the frog. Surfer Moe—isn't it silly?"

Perry raised a cushion and an eyebrow. "Did I say anything?"

"And now they're all gone, but it still makes me sad, you know? Like, when you're little it's another world or something, and you can't go back there *ever again,* no matter how much you want to." Future Holly searched the hillside. MapHead—invisibly—met her eyes. "I don't know what made me think about it. Jack's going to laugh when I tell him."

"When's he coming?"

"Next week. They're bringing *piles* of stuff for the baby. I'm an auntie now, you know. The baby's named Boothe, he's gorgeous. Jack says he's teething now, so I might stay on to help out."

"Auntie Holly. Do me a favor." Perry threw his cushion.

Auntie Holly. Future Jack. With—*baby Boothe?*—and all the family. MapHead quailed. Too much knowledge, too soon.

"No! Perry! Don't!" Future Holly dodged, shrieking, round the pool. Perry pelted after her. In moments they were splashing in the water.

MapHead watched the fun. Future rules had a kind of logic about them. It was good that he wasn't supposed to see too much. All he had to do was stick to the rules. Somewhere, Future MapHead waited. But not even Powers could look into his own future. MapHead would have to *live* it.

"I'm getting out! Perry! It's cold!" Future Holly swatted Perry with her towel. MapHead approved. With her berry bright eyes and her rich laugh, Holly had the crackle of a real live wire, one that would never be dampened by anything life might throw at it.

What would Jack Stamp—the Jack Stamp he knew—have made of Future Holly? Map-Head wondered. "Hey," he'd have said, "is she good for a loan? Are we ready to make some cash, or are we ready?" Maybe he'd've made her a special Jack Stamp Rap—"Holly with the Lolly," who knows? MapHead smiled, remembering. He pictured Jimmy-Jack Stamp lovingly reunited with his family, hugging them all in turn, his family hugging him back. He pictured Jack Stamp fitting in, and it didn't hurt at all for some reason.

Sorry I mixed you up, Jack Stamp. I won't be back for a long time. And then maybe only in your mind. I'm just so glad we saved Holly. Holly makes up for everything.

Holly was the silver lining. Family life, relationships, you name it. It all boiled down to much the same thing, in the end. These were the things that were important. Map-Head watched as the laughing girl on the patio pulled on a sweater and disappeared into the cool gloom of Casa Mañana with her friend. The wind had picked up quite a bit. Probably he should be going. A beach ball blew on the pool. The plants knocked gently together. *I see you, Future Holly. I know you don't see me.* MapHead waited, but she didn't come back. Still he felt OK. *I have knowledge to understand. I'm lonely, but not alone. . . .*

I see now. I understand. Suddenly Map-Head rose. *Dad! My task! I am it! I know how to choose between right and wrong, and Jack, my friend, helped me learn. My power and choice. My future.*

Anything was possible. MapHead's unimaginable future stretched away in front of him, its every moment boundless. The choice was his. No limits. Anything he wanted to be.

For a while, he'd been Pete Burns. What was the real Pete Burns like? MapHead wondered. Probably he liked a stiff drink while he was cooking. Probably he was wild haired, with eyebrows that met in the middle and bits of fish in his beard. Probably he could make Turbot Terrine or Salmon Mousse or Fried Excalibur Bananas. But could he wizard the future? Make the mountain come to Mohammed? Be all the things he wanted to be and *still* have room to learn?

MapHead glowed with satisfaction. He might not be a seafood chef who could whip up a Herring Supreme, but in or out of the kitchen, there were other fish he could fry. In full possession of his kingdom, MapHead looked down and knew. Half human but with power he knew what to do with, truly terrifying, his own best creation was himself.

Hey, Jack Stamp. You and me. This is goodbye for now. Thanks for showing me what families do. I learned more than you ever did. I used to be Boothe. Then Pete Burns. Who will I be next?